Dragonfire

Dragonfire

Anne Forbes

Kelpies

Kelpies is an imprint of Floris Books

First published in Kelpies in 2006
Published in 2006 by Floris Books
Copyright © 2006 Anne Forbes

The publisher acknowledges a Lottery grant
from the Scottish Arts Council towards the
publication of this series.

British Library CIP Data available

ISBN-10 0-86315-552-9
ISBN-13 978-086315-552-9

Produced in Poland by Polskabook

For my mother, who loved Edinburgh

Contents

Prologue	9
1. Jarishan	13
2. Amgarad Attacks	19
3. Faery Tales	25
4. The Great Whisky Robbery	29
5. Past Times	35
6. Secret Passages	41
7. The MacArthurs	47
8. Rothlan's Story	53
9. The Dragon's Lair	57
10. Pigeon Post	61
11. Plots And Plans	67
12. Operation Arthur	73
13. Firestones	79
14. The Loch Ness Monster	85
15. Summer in Jarishan	93
16. Emergency Flight	99
17. Magic Carpets	109

18. Mischief the Cat   115

19. Nightmare Times   125

20. The Pickpocket   131

21. Mobiles and Merging   141

22. The Edinburgh Tattoo   147

23. Kidnapped   155

24. Dragonfire   161

25. Preparations for War   171

26. Journey to Jarishan   179

27. The Storm Carriers   183

28. Clara's Adventure   191

29. Amgarad's Agony   199

30. Dragonsleep   205

31. Battle of the Giants   215

32. Healing Hexes   223

33. Prince Kalman   229

34. A Matter of Time   237

35. Here Be Dragons   245

Prologue

Had you seen him striding determinedly across the heather-clad landscape you would probably have guessed that he was a wizard or magician, for there was something indefinably evil and oppressive about the tall figure that strayed neither right nor left as it climbed to the summit of the hill. Darkness seemed to cling to him and black clouds gathered and swirled in the sky above as he took the slope in long, even strides.

Despite the deep-brimmed black hat pulled down over his face, the black crow that clung to his shoulder and the long, black coat that flapped around his legs as he walked, he did not look particularly wizard-like. Perhaps it was the opaque grey mist that gave the clue, drifting eerily in the gloom as though a thousand ghosts had risen to pay him homage. Had you been there, you would surely have shrunk in terror as the power of an unspoken evil threaded the thin folds of the mist; an evil that was reflected in his malevolent gaze. For the tall figure standing at the top of the hill was none other than Prince Kalman Meriden of Ardray, one of the most powerful magicians in Scotland.

From the hilltop, the prince gazed over a grim, lonely valley where snow lay thick on the ground and the black waters of a broad river ran deep. As his eyes lifted beyond its banks, he gave a nod of satisfaction. It was as he had expected; for before him lay a magic land, a land where the sun did not shine and the snows of countless winters drifted thick and deep over moor and mountain. Jarishan, the home of his hated enemy, Lord Rothlan.

"The magic shield is still in place, Kitor," he said, addressing the crow. "A pity that I will have to break it to get in, but there is no choice." He paused to look searchingly across the deserted landscape. "But it will only be for a few minutes. Once I am inside, it can be restored immediately and then we can begin our search."

Slowly the prince raised his arms, stiffened his fingers and chanted the words of a powerful spell. A deafening crack screamed through the high mountains on the far side of the river and for an instant they seemed to shiver and fragment, as though shaken to their age-old roots. The magician surveyed the scene through watchful eyes; for as the mountains settled and stilled, an invisible hand seemed to pass over their jagged heights and removed what looked like a grimy, grey film from their slopes, leaving the snowy peaks sharp and bright in the clear air. The magic shield that had surrounded Jarishan for centuries was broken!

With a cruel smile on his lips he reached out his arm to cast another hex and although his voice was softer this time, the second spell was just as powerful as the first. Hardly had his words ceased echoing round the valley than there was a sinister rustling and tumbling in the heather around him and from among its tough, sinewy roots appeared hundreds of strange creatures: small, grey and shiny black. They glistened wetly in the mist, their dome-like heads pierced by round, red eyes, their mouths rubbery slits and their ears like the gills of fish. Such were the water goblins that Prince Kalman had called from the watery depths of Scotland's lochs to do his bidding.

Once more the dark prince gazed across the valley to the cold mountain peaks that lay before him and cast a third spell; a spell that hid him and his water goblins from the eyes of the magical world. Now, no crystal ball would see them moving downhill to the river; neither would they be seen crossing it.

Prince Kalman smiled in triumph. Jarishan was open to him at last.

1. Jarishan

However hard you try and however closely you look, you will not find Jarishan on any map of Scotland. Jarishan is a magical place and lies, it is said, somewhere on the west coast among the heather-clad hills of Moidart. No one has seen Jarishan for many a long year, for it is a cold, icy place, the home of storms, mists and monsters.

It is also home to a magician, Lord Rothlan, who lives on an island in the middle of Jarishan Loch. His castle, tall and turreted, is surprisingly elegant and in happier days when the sun was allowed to shine, was the envy of the less fortunate. Now its walls are dark, stained and cold; the golden days of summer but a memory. Lord Rothlan rarely thinks of them and, if he does, it is with anger and a desire for revenge; for over the years he has become dark and bitter. Yet he was not always so and there are those among the Lords of the North who still remember his charm and ready laughter.

His crime, however, had been unforgivable. Hundreds of years before, Rothlan had betrayed his fellow magicians and the ruling against him had been harsh. A magic shield had been placed around his lands; a shield that had kept him, and his people, prisoners within its invisible walls. He had not only been banned from the world of magic and magicians, but his domain had also been deprived of all seasons except winter. His once proud eagles shared his punishment and had been transformed into fearsome monsters, their feathers rank and foul. Rothlan felt his enforced loneliness severely and

his anger had grown with the passing of the years until
he had become a proud and vengeful lord.

Wrapped in robes of fur he spent the days and years
of his exile perusing volume after volume of dusty,
ancient tomes that had accumulated in his library
over the centuries. Many charms were already known
to him, and all wizards, faeries and goblins can merge
with humans, birds and animals. From the crabbed
writing that covered the yellowing pages of his books,
however, he gleaned many darker, long-forgotten spells
and enchantments.

The years passed and by the dawn of the twenty-first
century, Lord Rothlan was not only more vengeful but
also a magician of considerable ability. He spent much of
his time reading in his study; a grand, richly-furnished
room dominated by a glittering crystal ball. For hundreds of years the ball had revealed nothing more than a
white swirling mist that hid the world of magic from his
sight, and so accustomed was he to its opaque emptiness
that he had come to regard it as an ornament rather
than a means of communication.

The crystal, however, still retained its power and
as Prince Kalman broke the shield that surrounded
Jarishan, he unwittingly brought it back to life.

Lord Rothlan lifted his head sharply from his book
as he became aware of a low, but hauntingly familiar,
humming noise. So long was it since he had last heard
the sound that it took him a few seconds to place it, and
when he did, the shock totally unnerved him. The globe
was no longer dead but glowing with life and pulsating
with energy.

Shaking with emotion, Lord Rothlan rose from his
chair. With trembling fingers he drew close and, touching
the crystal ball lightly, gasped as he felt the old, familiar
surge of power run through him. Avidly he stared into

the crystal as he had in times long past. It was clear ...
clear! No longer cloudy it glowed with a weird, unearthly
light and in its depths he glimpsed fabulous jewels and
vague figures. As he caught his breath in recognition
they disappeared, blotted out by streaking, yellow and
red flames, that for brief seconds curled round the inside
of the glass. It was over in minutes. To his dismay the
crystal started to fade and as it dulled, the mist returned
and the crystal clouded over once more.

"Amgarad!" called Lord Rothlan, striding up and
down the room in his excitement. "Am – garad!"

His voice reached the topmost turret of the castle
where Amgarad, captain of the eagles, had his nest.
Hearing the unaccustomed urgency in his master's
voice, the bird lifted his head sharply from the protection of his nest and flinched as a bitter wind, laced
with the promise of snow, struck his unprotected head.
Although the turret commanded a superb view of the
surrounding area, it was hardly the most desirable of
residences. Open to the four winds, its slit windows had
no glass and there was little protection from the biting
cold that penetrated every corner of the tower.

"Amgarad!" the call came again, more urgently.

Suppressing a sigh, for he had just managed to settle himself in a comfortable position, the monstrous
bird lifted one talon after another and, with a careful
delicacy born of long practice, clawed his way out of the
mountain of sticks and thorns that served as his nest.
With a flap of wings, he landed on one of the stone win-
dowsills, teetering on its brink for a few seconds before
plunging into the void.

Amgarad appeared at his best when in flight. He was
an impressive sight with huge, black wings feathered
against the rising air currents that allowed him to
soar and swoop effortlessly over loch and mountain.

Seen close, however, there was little about him that was noble. Despite his strong, hooked beak, he was an object of disgust; an evil hag of a bird whose rank, fretted feathers hung about him like a foul cloak.

Seconds later, in a flurry of wings, he landed on the windowsill of Lord Rothlan's study and swooped to a perch near his master's chair. Rothlan closed the window behind him and turned, his lips thinning in disgust as he viewed the dreadful bird. Meeting his glance, Amgarad closed his eyes in shame and hung his head. He opened them to find his master standing before him, his eyes understanding and blazing with a fire that he had not seen in years.

His handsome face was, nevertheless, grim and angry. "I have never forgiven them for what they did to you, Amgarad. I suffer for you, believe me!" Striding over to the crystal, he stroked its smooth surface and his voice, when he spoke, was harsh and triumphant. "But it may well be, Amgarad, that our days in exile are coming to an end! And when I have my power back, how I shall make them all pay!"

"Master?" Amgarad's voice trembled with hope. "How ... how can that be?"

"The crystal, Amgarad! The crystal came to life this afternoon! Only for a short time but I saw in it those that I recognized!" He strode up and down the room trying to contain his excitement.

"Prince Kalman?" The great bird croaked horribly.

"No," Rothlan frowned and shook his head at the mention of the name, "not Kalman Meriden. No, strangely enough, Amgarad, I saw the MacArthurs." He shot the bird a keen glance. "You remember them? From Edinburgh?"

As Amgarad nodded, Rothlan spoke thoughtfully. "I saw the MacArthurs amid fire and flames. And I saw firestones lying on a heap of treasure." He pursed his lips. "Could they be the stones that hold the magic shield in place around us?" He shook his head doubtfully. "Something is happening in the world outside our realm and whatever it is, it must be to our benefit; otherwise why would the crystal reveal it to me?"

He paced the floor and then stopped decisively in front of the bird. "I will consult with Hector and the rest of my captains, but first of all I must know why my crystal has suddenly come to life. You must act as my eyes and ears, Amgarad. Something strange is going on and if the crystal does not lie then it may well concern those in the hill at Holyrood. I am relying on you to find out."

"Holyrood! You mean that I am to fly to Edinburgh, master? But ... but how can I ...?"

"The crystal gave me power, Amgarad. Not a great deal, the time was too short, but I have enough to break the magic ring that surrounds us. Enough to let you through."

Amgarad took a deep breath and drew himself up proudly. "Master, I will go. Only tell me who or what I must find and I shall do my best."

Rothlan sat in his great chair and surveyed the bird sombrely. "Come, perch here on the arm of my chair. Your journey will be long and there is much that I must tell you before you leave Jarishan."

Night fell and servants came in to mend the fire and light the candles long before Lord Rothlan had finished instructing Amgarad. The sight of master and bird in deep conclave caused them to exchange glances and it was not long before a new spirit of anticipation entered the castle as whispered words spread an air of optimism.

2. Amgarad Attacks

If you lived in Edinburgh, you would know that at the entrance to Holyrood Park, just inside the gates of the park itself, there is a pretty stone cottage, which is the home of one of the Park Rangers. Behind this cottage sweeps the immensity of the park itself and the slopes of one of Edinburgh's most prominent features; a high hill, shaped like a sleeping dragon that is known locally as Arthur's Seat.

The Ranger's children, Neil and Clara, had spent much of their childhood roaming the park with their father. They knew its every nook and cranny, and over the years had learned many of its secrets.

In fact, while Amgarad winged his way silently eastwards, Ranger MacLean's two children were having a fierce, whispered argument, as they did not want their parents to hear what they were planning; or rather, what Neil was planning. Clara, who was afraid of the dark, was appalled at Neil's scheme. She heard him out in silence and found that her hands were shaking.

"You've got to be joking, Neil," she whispered. "You know what the park is like at night! Full of tramps and weirdos! Mum will go mental!"

"Chill, Clara! We've no choice! We've got to go, and it's got to be tonight. They've stopped coming out during the day; I've been looking out for them for ages and they're just not around anymore. Not Jaikie, not Hamish ... not even Archie!"

"Do you think it has anything to do with the noises we heard?"

"I'm sure it has! That's why we've got to go to the well. We have to find out what's going on!"

"I'm scared, Neil! You know I hate the dark! And I just have a bad feeling about going out on the hill tonight."

"I'll go on my own if you don't come," her brother promised. "It's not only the noises, you know. It's the birds and the sheep! They're really nervous and as jittery as anything."

Clara bit her lip. Neil was right. There was something strange going on in the park. "Okay, I'll come with you," she said decisively, "but only because I'd be just as nervous here, waiting for you to come back."

Neil's face lit up. "Great! I knew you wouldn't let me down. Come on, let's get ready for bed so that Mum will think we've gone to sleep when she comes in."

Midnight saw the house dark and silent as the two children struggled into their clothes, trying to make as little noise as possible. Clara had almost fallen asleep as, one by one, the familiar noises of the house gradually ceased but excitement had kept Neil awake as he thought out the route they would take to the old ruin beside St Anthony's Well where they had first heard the disturbing, dark rumblings.

"Did you put out the torches, Neil?" whispered Clara, poking her head round the door of his room.

"Yes. Here, where are you? Hold out your hand!"

Clara fumbled for the proffered torch and zipped it into the pocket of her jacket. Neil was excited but she had a premonition of danger and fear gripped her.

Just after midnight, when they were creeping down the garden path and slowly opening the garden gate that still squeaked despite their care, Amgarad swept on silent wings over the two brightly-lit bridges spanning the Firth of Forth.

Amgarad's journey had not been without incident, and he had endured much since leaving Jarishan. Brave of heart and accustomed to being the undisputed master of the skies, he had unhesitatingly taken on all the strange monsters that had crossed his path during his flight and in doing so had done much to endanger life and limb. After a near-fatal encounter with a helicopter that had left him short of more than a few tail feathers, he had proceeded to take on an articulated lorry with equally disastrous results. Reduced to a trembling but undaunted bundle of feathers, it had taken him some time to recover but, as a result, his approach to the unknown was now more circumspect.

He regarded the two bridges over the Firth of Forth with deep suspicion and hesitated. Finally, he circled wide to avoid observation, for in front of him lay the glittering vista that marked his destination — Edinburgh!

Looking in amazement at the swathes of light that lit up the night sky he felt a creeping sense of bafflement and unease. Since leaving Jarishan, it had not taken him long to realize that the world had changed considerably. Grimly he hoped that Edinburgh's old town would still be as he remembered it; a motley jumble of tall tenements between which ran alleys and ancient closes that hid secrets and, more importantly, offered shelter to the hunted.

Tired after his long flight and more than a little afraid of being seen, his sharp eyes scanned the grey water below, seeking a resting place on one of the tiny islands in the firth. A ruined abbey showed briefly against the silver water and feathering his wings slightly, he edged towards it. Dark, deserted and safe from prying eyes it would serve his purpose. He landed on a broken ledge and rested gratefully while considering his next move.

No longer, it seemed, could he rely on total darkness to conceal him; the unexpected brightness of so many lights was a problem that neither he nor his master had either envisaged or expected but there were other ways of travelling unseen. Silently, he launched himself over the sea, uttering a dreadful cry that echoed dismally over the waves and struck fear into the hearts of some nesting gulls. As he glided low over the water, the sea beneath him began to bubble and froth, and gave off a dense white mist that rose and began to roll in billowing clouds towards Edinburgh.

Neil and Clara did not notice the mist at first as they were too busy climbing the steep hillside towards the well. They soon realized to their horror that even with their torches on, they could barely see a few feet in front of them.

"Neil, this isn't funny," Clara gasped, looking round at the thick whiteness that surrounded them. "Where's the well?"

"A bit to the right, I think. Look, I'll lead the way and you hold on to my jacket. It's not that much further."

Gingerly they moved forward, step by step, and it was more by luck than judgment that Neil found the old stonework surrounding the well. They peered through the grating into its depths, but there was little to see apart from struggling clumps of ferns and grasses. The hill was eerily silent with no sound apart from the steady drip of moisture to comfort them.

Suddenly, Clara grasped Neil by the arm. "I heard something," she whispered. "No, not from the well," she muttered as Neil leant over to listen. "Over there ... shhhhh ... There's someone over there, in the mist!"

On impulse she picked up a piece of broken rock that lay nearby; it was a weapon of sorts if anyone threatened them. Shivering with fear, she crouched by the well, and had just pulled Neil down beside her when a roar of sound erupted from its depths. They leapt to their feet in fright at precisely the same moment that Amgarad, talons outstretched and wings flapping, swooped down to land opposite them.

It is difficult to say who got the greater fright. Amgarad had certainly not expected to meet anyone at that time of night and after the initial shock saw, to his relief, that his adversaries were merely children. Spreading his wings, he dived at them, his talons ripping the sleeve of Neil's jacket and his beak tearing at its hood.

Clara turned to run but then remembered the rock she held in her hand. Screaming at the top of her voice, she threw it at Amgarad and had the satisfaction of seeing him jerk in pain. He loosened his grip on Neil's jacket and his black, angry eyes turned upon her.

"Run, Clara!" Neil shouted as he rushed at Amgarad, trying to pinion his wings. The strength of the bird was too much for him, however. Amgarad shrugged him off and, with a dreadful cry, knocked him to the ground and held him with one of his talons.

"Neil! Clara! Where are you?" The Ranger's voice rang out through the mist.

"Here, Dad, here!" screamed Clara.

Amgarad's head lifted as he heard the Ranger's voice. The man was too close. Reluctantly he left Neil, flapped heavily into the air and disappeared into the mist.

"Neil, are you all right?" Clara sobbed as she ran up. "Dad's here. I heard him!"

"Dad! Dad! Over here!" Neil shouted.

"What was it?" gasped Clara. "It was awful. I've never seen a bird like that before. It had a beak like an eagle but its feathers were like ... dirty rags!"

At that moment the Ranger loomed through the fog. Clara threw herself into his arms. "Oh Dad!" she cried. "A bird attacked us!"

"A bird! Is that what the noise was?" said the Ranger. "Good grief, Neil! Look at your jacket!"

"Never mind my jacket, Dad! Listen here, at the well. What do you think is making that noise?"

The Ranger leant over the well and listened to the strange roars, rumblings and hissings that rose from its depths. "That's strange," he said looking puzzled. "I don't understand it. I'll come up here tomorrow when it's light and have a scout round. And if I see the bird that did that to your jacket, Neil, I'll shoot it!"

Amgarad, hunched on a nearby rock, heard his last remark and smiled nastily. Good luck to him! As he heard them making their way down the slope through the swirling mist, he returned to the well and listened with interest to the noises that emanated from it.

3. Faery Tales

The lights were on in the cottage. "Is Mum up?" Clara asked.

"Yes," answered their father. "She heard the gate creak and woke me up. You have some explaining to do, the pair of you!"

Mrs MacLean was furious when they arrived, wet and bedraggled, at the door of the cottage. Her anger, however, quickly changed to concern when she saw how tired both children looked.

"Take off your things and ...! Neil MacLean! What have you done to your jacket? Look at it! Ripped to pieces!"

John MacLean shook his head. "We'll go into that later, Janet," he said warningly. "Now Neil, I want to hear the whole story right from the beginning. Your mother and I are listening."

Neil looked at them doubtfully. "I don't quite know where to start," he admitted. "Really, it's to do with the MacArthurs. The ... the little people that live in the hill."

Janet MacLean looked at her son with startled eyes. "What are you talking about, Neil? People that live in the hill? *In Arthur's Seat?*" she said disbelievingly. "Don't talk rubbish!"

"Honestly, Mum!" I know it sounds crazy but there *are* people that live in the hill. They call themselves the MacArthurs. Clara and I have known them for years and we still see them sometimes; not as often as we used to, 'cos we've got school and homework and stuff, but they've always been around. They're our friends!"

"And ... er ... just how did you meet them?" asked his father.

"I don't really know. They just always seemed to be around when we were exploring the hill. We knew they were different but we were young then and didn't think that much about it."

"We just thought they were funny," Clara interrupted. "They could change themselves into birds and animals, you see. If anyone appeared suddenly, they would merge into whatever animal was nearby — a sheep or rabbit or anything. Even a bird. They could still talk to us, though."

"It's true, Dad!" Neil nodded. "They can do magic!"

His father heaved a sigh. "You don't have to convince me," he said quietly. "I know all about the MacArthurs."

"You know *what?*" His wife looked utterly flabbergasted. "Don't be ridiculous, John! We've lived here for years! How on earth can there be people living in the hill that I don't know about?"

The Park Ranger sighed. "You remember that bad winter we had a few months before Neil was born?"

"Of course I remember it! You nearly died rescuing some sheep on the hill! Do you think I'll ever forget it? You fell down a cliff!"

"I should have told you at the time but I ... well, quite frankly, I thought that if I told you there were faeries living in Arthur's Seat you'd have thought that the bang I got on my head had scrambled my brains!"

"Faeries? Neil didn't say anything about faeries!"

"It's what my father used to call them. He was Park Ranger before me, remember? He told me about them. According to him, they've always lived in Arthur's Seat."

"You've known about them all along, Dad?" Clara sat up, her eyes accusing. "And you never told *us!*"

"Well, I didn't know that you had anything to do with them, did I? And if I'd started talking about faeries living in Arthur's Seat, you'd probably have thought I'd gone crazy!"

"What happened, Dad?" asked Neil curiously.

"They saved my life, that's what happened. I slipped and fell down a cliff when I was bringing in some sheep. It was pitch black and there was a blizzard. I more or less knocked myself out when I fell and I'd have died in a snow drift if they hadn't rescued me. I only came round when I was half way home and after what my father had said ... well, I just knew it was them. Your mother thought I'd made my own way back but the truth is that they carried me."

"You should have told me, John," his wife said sharply. "When I opened the door that night I thought I saw some people on the road outside. They had sheepskin jackets on, I remember, but I was so upset at finding you the way I did that all I could think of was getting you to the hospital."

"They must have been MacArthurs, then," Clara nodded. "That's what they wear — sheepskin jackets over leggings and tunics."

"All this, though," interrupted her father, "doesn't explain why you had to leave the house tonight and go up to the well!"

"It was my fault, Dad. Clara didn't want to come."

"But why, Neil? Why go in the first place?"

"I told you. It was because of the MacArthurs. They've stopped coming out onto the hill and ... well, I don't know how to explain it, but there's a strange atmosphere up there just now."

His father nodded. "I've noticed it too," he admitted.

"The animals are jumpy, the geese and swans have left the lochs and now there are those weird noises ..."

"Not only from the well," asserted Neil, "but from other places too. Something's going on inside the hill, Dad, and I'm worried about them."

"I don't know whether to believe you or not," muttered his mother, running her hands through her hair.

"I'm sure they're in trouble, Mum. I thought they might be coming out of the hill in the dark instead of the daylight. That's why we went to the well!"

"Tell me about the bird now," said his father.

"It was a horrible thing, Dad," interrupted Clara. "It was as big as an eagle and had a beak like an eagle, but it was more like a vulture with horrible droopy feathers. And its claws!" she shuddered. "It would have attacked me if Neil hadn't grabbed it!"

"I think," interrupted Neil, "that it got as much of a fright as we did. I don't think it expected to see anyone at the well and it wanted to scare us off!"

"It was a bird, Neil! You're talking about it as though it were a person!"

"I know," agreed Neil. "But there was something about its eyes. I wonder if it really was a bird."

"You really never can tell with the MacArthurs," Clara nodded seriously.

"And on that note," said her mother firmly, "we are all going to bed for what is left of the night!"

4. The Great Whisky Robbery

The following morning, the mist still crept, thick and heavy, through the streets of Edinburgh, chilling its inhabitants as it billowed in from the sea. In the middle of town the solid bulk of Edinburgh Castle, perched on its massive rock, might well not have been there for all that could be seen of it.

Despite the mist, the castle that morning was a hive of activity as preparations were in full swing for the most important event in its calendar: the Edinburgh Military Tattoo.

In a rich, panelled room inside the castle itself, a committee meeting was just breaking up.

"Well, gentlemen," remarked its chairman, Lord Harris, slipping a pile of papers into his briefcase, "I think we can congratulate ourselves this year. We are well ahead of schedule and apart from the moving walkways that the French are insisting upon, there doesn't really seem to be much that's problematic!" He looked round the table appreciatively. "I must thank you all for your hard work, gentlemen. It's because of your individual skills and expertise that we have made such a good team. I'm sure that Sir James will agree with me."

Sir James Erskine who, as commentator for the Tattoo, had been invited to sit in on the meeting, nodded his head in agreement, as they packed up and moved towards the door.

"Good heavens!" exclaimed one of the committee. "The mist is still hanging around! Let's hope the weather is a bit better when the performances begin!"

"Early days yet, Cameron," replied Sir James.

"Whatever the weather," interrupted Lord Harris, "I'm sure you'll sail through it all magnificently, James. Isn't this your fifth year of giving the commentary? It must be pretty nerve-wracking for you up there in the commentary box."

"Yes," agreed Sir James, "I enjoy it, but I must admit that there are times when I wonder why I ever volunteered for the job. If anything goes wrong it can be a nightmare! I always have a fund of stories ready in case I have to fill in any gaps."

"Where are these moving walkways for the French horsemen going to be installed?" Lord Harris asked as they reached their cars.

"For the Spahis? Round about here," Cameron indicated, "one on either side of the esplanade. Just a few yards from the audience."

"Is that wise having the horses so close to the crowds?"

"The problem is space. Customs and Excise have a team of precision marchers and their leader ... what's his name ...?"

"Dougal MacLeod, isn't it?" frowned Lord Harris.

"That's it, Dougal MacLeod. Yes, well, he said that they wouldn't have enough room if the walkways were any closer."

Sir James smiled wryly. "He and Colonel Jamieson almost came to blows about it, I understand. MacLeod's always been a bit of a stickler. Actually he's due at the distillery today to make one of his inspections so I'll be seeing him later. I'll mention it to him, but he isn't the most co-operative of people."

"In my opinion, it would be better if we didn't have these walkways at all!" Lord Harris muttered. "They're too close to the audience for comfort and in my experience anything involving animals is an open invitation to disaster. Do they really need them?"

"Well, you know the outline of the pageant," Cameron said patiently. "The Touareg attack the desert fort and capture the women, and the Spahis want to give the impression of galloping miles across the desert to the rescue — hence the moving walkways. I understand they're using one in France to practise on so that the horses will be used to them by the time they arrive."

"Hmmm!" Lord Harris was not impressed. "Hope it's not a disaster!"

Sir James, however, had every faith in the horsemanship of the Spahis and left the castle feeling cheerful and quite up-beat about his role in the forthcoming Festival.

Sir James's distillery was one of the few privately-owned distilleries in Scotland. A high-walled, rather ugly building made from old, grey stone, it nestled unobtrusively among the lower slopes of Holyrood Park and was completely overshadowed by the eye-catching grace of its neighbour, Holyrood Palace.

As Sir James drew up in the cobbled forecourt of the distillery, his heart sank as he saw a car emblazoned with the insignia of HM Customs and Excise parked beside the office block. MacLeod had already arrived!

The feeling of anxiety that crept over him was compounded by the strange behaviour of his secretary, who, unaccountably flustered, met him on the stair.

"Thank goodness you're here, Sir James," she whispered. "I thought I'd warn you! The Excise man arrived early and there seems to be something wrong with the vats."

"Thank you, Janice," he murmured, holding the door open for her. "Where is Mr MacLeod now?"

"He's in the waiting room, Sir. I gave him a cup of coffee."

"Better make me some too please, Janice," her boss rejoined, "and ask Jamie Todd to come up as soon as he can, so that we can sort things out."

He walked to the waiting room where the lanky figure of Dougal MacLeod sat hunched over a pocket calculator. The Excise man was a tall, hatchet-faced man with a beak of a nose and bushy, sandy eyebrows. He had eyes like gimlets that seemed strangely triumphant. Sir James felt a prickle of fear as he strode forward, nerves making his voice sound friendlier than usual.

"Sorry I'm late, Dougal," he said as he shook hands. "I'm just back from the castle and we stopped by the esplanade to work out where they're going to put these walkways for the French contingent."

Dougal stiffened at the mention of the walkways. "I was going to mention it to you, Sir James, for that Colonel Jamieson was no help at all, at all! He did not seem to realize that we cannot be altering our routine to fit in with the French. Just a few feet, he kept saying! Even a few inches make a difference!"

Sir James had seen the Customs and Excise's team of precision marchers before and appreciated his argument. Dougal was not exaggerating when he said that inches mattered.

As he ushered MacLeod to his office, Janice entered with the coffee. "Mr Todd will be up in a minute, Sir," she said.

"Ah, thank you, Janice," he said, placing his cup on the coffee table. He waited for her to close the door before turning to MacLeod.

"Now, Dougal," he made his voice as casual as he could, "Janice mentioned something about one of the vats?"

Dougal MacLeod smiled. It was a smile that struck terror into Sir James's heart, for in all the time he had known him he had never seen Dougal MacLeod smile.

The Excise man was enjoying himself. This was his moment! There was no way that Sir James was going to talk himself out of *this!*

"Well, now, Sir James, I have to tell you that there is a considerable amount of whisky missing from your vats. A very considerable amount! In fact," he remarked with elaborate casualness, "I make it nearly twenty thousand gallons."

Sir James, who had just taken a sip of coffee, promptly choked into his cup. "What did you say?" he gasped, getting to his feet to wipe hot coffee from his impeccably cut suit. "*What* did you say?"

Dougal MacLeod eyed him dryly, quite aware of the bombshell he had just dropped. "Twenty thousand gallons of whisky are missing from your vats and you will agree, Sir James," he went on in his soft, Highland voice, "that twenty thousand gallons is a tidy amount of whisky! Enough for a small loch, you might say!"

Sir James eyed his adversary with extreme dislike, but twenty thousand gallons *was* a lot of whisky and how exactly it had disappeared was beyond him.

"Twenty thousand gallons!" he exclaimed incredulously. "Twenty thousand gallons! I don't believe it! You must have made a mistake! It's impossible!"

"It's not impossible, Sir James. It has happened. How it has happened I could not say but the fact remains that somehow, somebody is tapping your vats." For many years he had been trying to prove that there was steady pilfering going on. Where or how, he had never quite been able to find out, but he had always had his suspicions. His long nose twitched.

And now he had been proved right with a vengeance! "Maybe someone with a wee private pipeline of his own?" he suggested.

Sir James eyed him warily, conscious that he had broken out in a cold sweat. If only the man knew how right he was! But twenty thousand gallons was ridiculous! "We'll have to look into it, of course," he said. "Give me a few days to find out what's been going on and I'll ring you before the end of the week."

"Don't be leaving it too long, Sir James," the other remarked. "I have a report to make out, as you know."

Sir James rubbed his chin thoughtfully. "Hang fire for a while, Dougal, won't you. After all, it might just be that somebody got their sums wrong!"

"Not to the tune of twenty thousand gallons though, I'm thinking," was the Excise man's parting shot as he took up his cap and left the office, shutting the door gently behind him.

5. Past Times

Sir James let out a long breath and stared blankly at the dark, oak panelling that lined his office. He just couldn't get that dreadful amount out of his head. Twenty thousand gallons! It had never happened before. Something must be wrong, very wrong indeed. And how on earth was he going to explain it away this time? Pressing the intercom button, he spoke to his secretary. "Janice, what's happened to Jamie? I want to see him at once!"

When Jamie Todd, the Distillery Foreman, entered Sir James's office, he found his employer gazing out of the window at the red cliffs dominating the park.

"What the devil is going on, Jamie?" he asked, swinging round. "That Excise man has been ranting on about twenty thousand gallons of whisky having gone missing! Tell me it's not true!"

Jamie Todd ran a hand through his hair. "I'm afraid it is that, Sir James. I was going to phone you at the castle when I realized, but MacLeod arrived early. By my reckoning, two vats must have been emptied over the holiday and Number Three is only a quarter full."

"But they can't have taken that amount, surely?" muttered Sir James. "It's never happened before! They *know* we have to account for every drop! Dougal's been treating me like one of the Great Train Robbers for years and this time he's got me cold. How the devil are we going to explain away twenty thousand gallons of whisky?"

"We could always say the faeries took it!"

Sir James eyed him sourly. "If the faeries took it then there must be some very sore heads out there," he snapped. "But can we be sure that they have taken it?"

"Who else has access to the vats?"

"That's true," Sir James scratched his head. "I think, Jamie, that I'll have to get in touch with them somehow. Dougal MacLeod's deadly serious this time."

"Do you know where to go?"

"I thought, perhaps, there might be an entrance near the well — you know, St Anthony's Well. Have you ever tried to find out?"

"No, Sir, although I've always had the impression that there's something ... dreadful under Arthur's Seat."

Sir James frowned. "Your father gave you no hint as to what it might be?" he asked. "After all, he was the one that helped them with the pipeline."

Jamie Todd thought for a few seconds. "The old Park Ranger helped as well," he said eventually. "My father always said that *he* knew more about the MacArthurs than he cared to let on."

"But he died a while ago, didn't he?"

"Aye, but his son took over the job after him. Nice chap. I know him quite well. If anything's going on in the hill then I reckon MacLean will know about it."

"Do you think it'd be worth paying him a visit?" frowned Sir James.

"I'll give him a ring and ask him to drop by. I'm sure he won't mind and, with any luck, he might even know the way into the hill."

The Ranger, as it happened, was at home when Jamie called and, anxious to hear anything he could about the MacArthurs, arrived at the distillery ten minutes later.

Sir James took an immediate liking to the tall, weather-beaten man that Jamie ushered into his office.

"Ranger MacLean," he smiled, rising to his feet and shaking his hand firmly. "Nice to meet you." Suddenly Sir James was uncertain how to continue.

"It's all right, Sir James. I told John on the way up that we were losing a lot of whisky and that you wanted to ask him about the MacArthurs," Jamie said helpfully.

"You do know about the MacArthurs, then?" Sir James asked.

"Aye, my father told me about them and ten years ago they rescued me from a snowdrift. I owe them my life."

"What exactly do they look like?" asked Sir James curiously. "I've never seen any of them myself, you see, and well ... I've often wondered."

"You mean, do they have pointed ears and the like?" grinned the Ranger.

"Well ..."

Ranger MacLean shook his head. "Actually, they look pretty much like us, but smaller. Otherwise you'd never know the difference. What I've always wondered is how *your* father got involved with them in the first place."

Jamie Todd leant forward and put his cup and saucer on the table. "It all started when my father noticed that small quantities of whisky were going missing from one of the vats."

"So he told my father," continued Sir James, "and between them they set a trap to catch the thief. It was quite an ingenious arrangement and it worked with unexpected results because it wasn't a man they caught but one of the MacArthurs; a young chap wearing a sheepskin jacket. Well, by the time they had fished him out of the vat, you could smell the whisky off him at a hundred yards. My father said that if he hadn't been in the state he was in, he would never have taken them into the hill. But he did, and when they came out they were both changed men, weren't they, Jamie?" He looked to his foreman who nodded solemnly in agreement.

"Neither my father nor Jamie's ever told us what happened in there but from that day on they were firm friends with the little folk and helped them rig up a secret pipeline from the distillery into the hill. That's where your father came into the picture, I should imagine. Being Park Ranger they would have had to take him into their confidence. Of course, it has always involved us in a wee bit of double-dealing as far as Customs and Excise are concerned but they've never been able to prove anything ... although," and here he grinned wryly, "they've always had their suspicions. As I say, it hasn't been much over the years but today they found a big discrepancy, a big discrepancy indeed, and I don't mind admitting that I find it very worrying. In fact, if I don't manage to get in touch with them to find out what is happening I might well end up in prison."

The Ranger looked thoughtful. "There's something very strange going on inside Arthur's Seat, but to be quite honest with you, I have no idea what it is," he admitted frankly. "The children say that they haven't seen any of the MacArthurs for some time. All the ducks and geese have left the lochs and strange noises have been coming out of the well. I heard them myself last night."

"You heard noises from the well?"

"I did. The children went there on their own to see if the MacArthurs were only coming out onto the hill when it was dark. They were at the well when a huge bird appeared out of the mist and attacked them. I've been out on the hill all day trying to spot it in case it attacks anyone else.

"You don't by any chance know the way into the hill, do you?" asked Sir James.

"I don't, but Neil and Clara might."

"It's most important that I meet with them," stressed Sir James. "In all honesty, I face ruin if I don't."

"You said a *lot* of whisky had gone missing ...?" queried the Ranger.

"Twenty thousand gallons have gone missing!" said Sir James savagely.

The Ranger stared at him in disbelief. "Twenty thousand gallons!" he whispered in awe. "That's an awful lot of whisky!"

"Now do you understand why I have to talk to them?"

"I do that!" answered the Ranger.

"Can we ask your children where the entrance is then?"

The Ranger looked at his watch and got to his feet. "They'll be home from school by this time," he said. "Let's go!"

6. Secret Passages

Dawn was just breaking next morning when Neil and Clara, followed by Sir James, Jamie Todd and the Ranger, walked along a narrow path on the slopes of Arthur's Seat. Neil stopped from time to time as if to take his bearings and then, more confidently, moved off the path towards a rocky outcrop.

"I think it's over here, Dad. They always seemed to move towards this part of the cliff when we were leaving."

"Did you never think to look for the way in and try to explore on your own?" queried his father.

Neil pondered the question. "I think we always knew that if they had wanted us in the hill, they would have invited us."

The Ranger nodded in relief but, as they moved closer to the rocky outcrop, a growing sense of unease made him watchful. Although he saw nothing, his fears were not unfounded, for high above them, Amgarad watched with baleful eyes. From his rocky vantage point, he had viewed the little group with more than a passing interest for he was fairly sure that the two children were those he had attacked at the well. And when they rounded a jutting cliff and did not reappear on the other side, he sat up and took notice. Slowly he flexed his great wings, launched himself into space and swooped downwards.

It did not take him long to discover where they had gone. Walking awkwardly, for he was only comfortable in the air, he strutted and flapped his way among the boulders until he saw a dark entrance in the cliff face.

Triumph, mingled with a certain amount of relief, flooded through Amgarad, as his own search for the entrance had been fruitless and he had spent a tortured, sleepless night envisaging the terrible prospect of failure. Barely able to contain his excitement, he hopped nearer to the slit-like opening that gaped blackly between two broken slabs of stone and peered into the darkness beyond.

It was then that his resolve weakened, for Amgarad was a creature of the air and to venture through black, confining tunnels where his wings would not serve him, was anathema to him. As it was, he took one last look at the rising sun and bravely hopped forward. The men and children were, he knew, not far in front of him and only a few moments passed before he caught a glimpse of torchlight ahead. Thankfully, he took a deep breath and followed the light.

Inside the hill, the Ranger had taken over as leader. He had come armed with ropes and other items of climbing gear but so far they had proved unnecessary as the going was relatively easy. The passage was wide and sloped smoothly and steadily downwards, but its spaciousness soon gave way to smaller, narrower passages.

The Ranger stopped suddenly.

"What is it?" whispered Sir James.

"A flight of stairs," said the Ranger. Sir James moved up and saw a flight of steps in front of him that curved like a spiral stairway down through the rock. It seemed to go on forever and they were all more than slightly dizzy by the time they reached the last step. The staircase gave onto a large, high-roofed chamber in whose walls gaped the black openings of other tunnels.

Sir James glanced around the room. "Well," he asked, "where do we go from here?"

Wordlessly, the Ranger shone his torch downwards, revealing a pathway of little footprints that led to the right-hand tunnel.

"Let's go, then," instructed Sir James.

The new tunnel led them deeper into the heart of the mountain. Gradually its roof became lower and the men passed with no little difficulty beneath a few jutting outcrops of rock. Soon, however, it came to an end and opened to reveal a deep split in the hill whose sheer walls formed a gorge of such impenetrable blackness that the narrow shafts of torchlight made little impression on its depths. This fearful chasm was spanned by a narrow bridge that looped in a fantastic curve over the void. They had little choice but to cross it.

The Ranger took the coil of rope from his shoulder and, anchoring one end firmly to a jutting rock, he fastened it round each of them. Strung safely together, they crossed the fragile structure on their hands and knees. By the time they had all reached the other side they were totally exhausted and, by common consent, paused to take stock of their surroundings.

"I think we should have something to eat and drink before we go any further," the Ranger announced, heaving a heavy rucksack from his back.

Clara had the same feeling of dread that she had felt on the hill and looked round fearfully. For someone who was afraid of the dark, it was a very dark place. She could feel the darkness like a blanket ready to smother her in its soft folds. Hastily she turned her eyes to the comforting light of the torches and gratefully bit into a cheese sandwich.

"You okay, Clara?" Neil asked.

"I'm fine," she lied.

From the far side of the bridge, Amgarad watched hungrily as they ate, but it was only when they set off again and the dancing torchlight disappeared down the tunnel, that he glided over the chasm on silent wings to follow them further. At the entrance to this new tunnel, however, Amgarad paused. His sense of smell was more acute than that of humans and this tunnel spelt danger.

The Ranger pressed ahead, his torch revealing a worn trail of footprints that took them deeper and deeper into the hill. It was not long, however, before he started to become alarmed.

"I don't like this at all," he said, flashing his torch on the wall. "Look at the walls! They've been scorched by fire — and the deeper we go, the blacker they get!"

"I've heard that Arthur's Seat is an extinct volcano ..." Sir James broke off suddenly and grasped the Ranger's arm. "Look!" he whispered, "Look! One of the MacArthurs!"

The Ranger shone his torch on a smallish, slight, fair-haired young man whose eyes blinked in the glare of its powerful beam. He rushed towards them.

"Go back! Go back!" he cried. "Thank goodness I found you! It's dangerous here! Quickly! Back to the bridge!"

Such was the urgency in his voice that they all turned immediately and started back the way they had come. Behind them came a rumbling roar that made their blood curdle, followed by a dreadful wave of heat and smoke that left them gasping and panting.

"Faster! Faster!" screamed the MacArthur.

At last the bridge was reached. Choking and gasping for breath they made to cross but the little creature, its sheepskin jacket black and tattered, pulled them to one side ... just in time. As they pressed back against the rocky wall, a burst of flame shot through the tunnel opening; a sparkling, glittering stream of fire that held all the colours of the rainbow, threaded with stars of gold and silver. It was more marvellous than any firework display they had ever seen.

Amgarad paled. The secret of the hill was revealed to him and, as the flames subsided and the roaring died away, he melted silently into the darkness. He had heard and seen enough.

The Ranger switched on his torch with an unsteady hand while Sir James drew a handkerchief from his pocket and mopped his brow. Clara and Neil, however, were staring at the MacArthur. "Hamish!" they said together, "Hamish! What on earth is going on?"

Sir James looked back at the drift of smoke that still wreathed from the mouth of the tunnel. "What," he demanded chokingly, "was that?"

"That," answered Hamish, "was our dragon!"

"You have a dragon?" gasped Neil. "You ... you never told us!"

"A dragon?" Sir James almost dropped his torch. "Did ... did you say a dragon?"

"I did that! But you must all come with me. It isn't safe here and besides, the MacArthur himself will want to see you. Come! Follow me!"

7. The MacArthurs

Without giving them time to protest, Hamish set off at a brisk trot and led them through a further maze of tunnels until they saw lights ahead and emerged into a cave of cathedral-like dimensions. Lit by blazing torches the cavern was an Aladdin's Cave stacked with piles of old furniture, strange, iron-framed mirrors, lamps and what looked like hundreds of Persian carpets. These not only layered the floor of the cave but were also stacked in rolls against the walls, their colours giving a glowing richness to the overall bleakness of the cavern.

Most amazing, however, were the occupants of this vast hall, for it was full of milling groups of little people. Some were wrapped in blankets, others wore sheepskin jackets over long tunics and leggings, and many were gathered round a thin, wizened little old man seated on an enormous carved, wooden chair, banked up with cushions. Heavily booted and dressed in a dull red tunic covered by a long fleece coat, he stared imperiously over the crowd, and noticed the new arrivals immediately.

There was a sudden silence as everyone turned to stare and the crowds parted as they were taken straight to the chieftain.

With a sweeping gesture of his arm, their escort bowed low.

"MacArthur," he announced. "I found these people near the dragon's tunnel. I got them out just in time!"

The MacArthur looked grimly at the little group and then smiled. "I think I ken you. It's Sir James, isn't it? Sir James Erskine?" he queried.

Sir James's ability to handle delicate social situations seemed to have deserted him as he bowed awkwardly and agreed that he was.

"Aye," the MacArthur announced. "Aye! You have the look of your father about you. And your friends?"

"Ranger MacLean from the Park and his children ... and my foreman at the distillery, Jamie Todd. You will, perhaps, remember his father ...?"

"Aye, of course. We are deeply indebted to him. Come and sit by me and tell me what brings you here."

Chairs were hastily placed around the MacArthur's throne and a servant brought a heavy silver tray bearing a jug of clear water and some tall glasses.

Sir James regarded his glass thoughtfully. "I think, MacArthur," he said, "that you probably know why we are here. Shall we say our National Drink? And," and here he held up his glass, "I don't mean water."

The MacArthur drew himself up haughtily. "I hope, Sir James, that you are not accusing us of drinking the ... er ... produce of your distillery. For it's no' the case ... no' the case at all. We drink nothing but pure spring water!"

Sir James nodded. "I'm not accusing you of drinking my whisky, but if *you* aren't drinking it, then who is? Or have twenty thousand gallons of it just vanished into thin air?"

The MacArthur sat up abruptly. "Twenty thousand gallons! Is it as much as that?"

A wave of excited whispering arose from the ranks of the MacArthurs at this disquieting piece of information. When it died down, the MacArthur stroked his chin thoughtfully and gazed speculatively at Sir James.

"Then your father, Sir James, never told you why we rigged up yon wee pipeline?"

"No, he did not. I ... actually, I always assumed that you drank the whisky yourselves, but as I can see for myself that you don't, I'm prepared to accept that there might be another explanation."

"It so happens ..." The MacArthur tailed off as the sound of a tremendous roar echoed round the cavern, "... that there *is* a very good explanation. In fact, you have just heard it!"

The Ranger broke in, "Do you mean to say that it's the dragon that's ... that's ...?"

The MacArthur nodded sourly. "Aye!" he gestured angrily. "Uncontrollable! Fire and smoke all over the place, day in, day out until we're all sick of it." He stood up and waved his stick. "And do you know whose fault it is?" He paused dramatically and pointed. "His fault! He was the one that found a bottle of whisky on the hill and gave it to Arthur! Come forward Archie and let me introduce you!"

A shamefaced MacArthur moved forward and bowed low.

The MacArthur was fast working himself into a passion. "This miserable specimen is Mad Archie! And mad he is for only a lunatic, a fool, a jackass, a nincompoop, a complete and utter idiot would ever give a dragon whisky!

"I didn't know it was whisky, MacArthur!" whined the miserable specimen. "I thought it was some kind of tonic. And Arthur was that depressed, I just thought it might cheer him up a bit."

"Arthur?" questioned Sir James, looking vaguely round.

"Arthur," retorted the MacArthur, "is our dragon. And a decent, respectable dragon he was too until that idiot gave him whisky!"

"I'm sorry, Sir James' Archie said. "The thing is that Arthur is no fool. He saw me turning on the tap every night when I went to top him up and ..."

"Top him up? You mean ... you gave him a nightcap or something?"

The MacArthur laughed scornfully. "A nightcap! Dinna be daft! Dragons don't drink whisky. Any fool knows that!"

Sir James sat up with a pained expression on his face. "Then what *does* he do with it?"

The MacArthur shook his head in disbelief. "Think about it!"

Sir James looked baffled. "I'm sorry to appear so dense but I've rarely thought of dragons since I was about ten years old."

"Humph! Well, that would account for your not knowing!"

"Not knowing what?" interjected the Ranger quickly.

The MacArthur looked cross. "Well, how else do you think dragons breathe fire and smoke ... a wee dram of whisky and ... wrooooosh!"

There was a stunned silence as Sir James, the Ranger, Jamie Todd and the children assimilated this astounding piece of information.

"You see," explained the MacArthur in a reasonable voice, "Arthur's still a young dragon and it'll be a while yet before he can breathe fire on his own. He's always been a bit lonely, cooped up in the hill with only us for company, and it was when we found out how much he enjoyed blowing fire and smoke up from the bottle that Archie gave him that we started taking small amounts from your father's distillery, Sir James. Until, that is, Archie got caught and brought your father and Mr Todd into the hill. It was then that I had my great idea and we managed to persuade your father to set up the wee pipeline. To keep Arthur happy."

Sir James shook his head in disbelief. "The last thing my father would do is set up a pipeline of free whisky just to indulge a dragon in its favourite hobby."

The MacArthur shifted uncomfortably. "I explained the situation to Arthur, you see, and told him that if he acted his part well, the chances were that he would be able to 'top up' every night and blow fire and smoke to his heart's content for the rest of the day."

"And ...?" said Sir James faintly.

The MacArthur again looked uncomfortable. "We ... er ... spun your father and Mr Todd a tale about Arthur having woken up after five hundred years, and said we needed the whisky to keep him sedated, otherwise he would break out of the hill and terrorize the city."

"And my father believed that?" Sir James's voice was shrill with incredulity.

The MacArthur grinned reminiscently. "Oh aye! Arthur gave a fine performance ... a fine performance indeed. It frightened the wits out of me, I can tell you, and I've known Arthur for hundreds of years. He was worn out for days afterwards!"

Sir James burst out laughing. "Well, well, MacArthur," he chuckled. "You must be the only person in Edinburgh who ever got the better of my father."

"But why," persisted Jamie Todd, "did you decide to give Arthur thousands of gallons?"

"We didn't give it to him. Arthur watched Archie turn on the tap every night and decided to try it himself. He's got an absolute lake of the stuff down there."

"Aye," said Archie proudly, "he learned to turn the tap on himself."

"Then," said the MacArthur, "he wouldn't let us near it to turn it off again. By then he was having too much fun seeing how far he could throw the flames and ... well, to cut a long story short, he took to fire-raising in earnest. Look at us now! Living with the bits and pieces we could salvage in this cold, dark hall. He's burnt us out of house and hill!"

Sir James sighed and shook his head. "Well, if the tap is still turned on at the foot of his lake then I'm ruined. How the devil am I going to explain away twenty thousand gallons of whisky? What on earth am I going to do?"

"Disconnect the pipeline for a start," advised Jamie Todd. "Then at least it won't become thirty thousand gallons!"

"That's no good," opined the Ranger. "That would still leave twenty thousand gallons for the dragon to use up at his leisure. I'm thinking that it would be better for you to rig up some sort of pump at your end of the pipeline, Sir James, and pump back as much whisky as you can. You ought to be able to reclaim a tidy amount."

Sir James leapt to his feet and wrung the Ranger's hand. "Magnificent!" he cried. "Absolutely magnificent! I'll have my revenge on that Dougal MacLeod yet."

"Dougal MacLeod?" queried the MacArthur.

"The Excise man who thinks he's got me for stealing twenty thousand gallons of my own whisky! Now, don't worry, my dear sir," he said, "everything will sort itself out from now on. We'll rig a pump up right away to get our whisky back. No whisky for the dragon means no more fire and smoke to plague the life out of you. From now on, you'll have no more trouble from your dragon, I assure you!"

8. Rothlan's Story

A murmur of approval and relief greeted Sir James's words and the MacArthur beamed happily at his assurances. However, as an air of confident optimism permeated the hall, the Ranger wondered rather hesitantly if he should bring up the appearance of the strange, black bird that had attacked Clara and Neil.

"There is one thing that hasn't been explained, MacArthur, and it may well have nothing to do with you," began the Ranger slowly, "but two nights ago, a great black bird attacked Neil and Clara while they were on the hill.

"It was a huge bird," Clara interrupted, pushing her brown hair behind her ears and fixing the MacArthur with her clear blue eyes, "like an eagle, but its feathers were ..." her nose wrinkled in disgust, "... they were horrible ... like dirty, smelly rags ..."

Her voice tailed off as she realized that silence had fallen throughout the great hall.

The MacArthur sat stiffly upright, a sudden, stern look on his face that frightened her. It was Hamish who eventually broke the silence.

"Amgarad!" he said aloud, in an awed whisper. "It must be. I can't quite believe it but ..." he looked round wildly, "she's describing Amgarad!" He looked at the MacArthur and threw out his hands in disbelief. "After all this time! Master, how is it possible?"

The MacArthur raised his hand to quieten the spate of words.

"First of all let us listen to what the Ranger has to say, Hamish," he said, turning to the Ranger, his face serious and strained. "Tell me the story of this attack, Ranger, and miss nothing out, for it's important that we hear every detail."

The Ranger retold the story of how he had followed the children and they, in turn, told their tale of the mist and the attack by Amgarad at the well.

"Was it only the bird you saw?" pressed the MacArthur. "You didn't see anyone else?"

As Neil shook his head the MacArthur sat back among the pile of cushions that heaped his chair and looked at Hamish thoughtfully.

"How very interesting that Amgarad should be here. I wonder how ... and why?"

"And Lord Rothlan?" queried Hamish, walking agitatedly up and down in front of him. "If one is here, then the other must be here, too."

"One would think so," frowned the MacArthur, stroking his chin thoughtfully, "and yet, perhaps not."

Sir James coughed. "Who is this Lord Rothlan? May we know?"

The MacArthur regarded him sombrely. "Alasdair Rothlan was, at one time, one of the most powerful and popular faery lords of the Highlands but he fell out of favour years ago when Prince Charles Edward Stuart came from France to claim the throne."

"The Jacobite Rebellion of 1745!" Neil interrupted.

"As you say," agreed the MacArthur. "The Jacobite Rebellion. Ach, it was ill-fated from the start and the Prince was badly advised but, as faeries, we naturally supported the Scottish House of Stuart. One of the Lords of the North, Kalman Meriden, was Bonnie Prince Charlie's strongest supporter, but Rothlan had no respect for the Prince and it was mainly because of

him that the rebellion failed. Kalman was furious with
Rothlan for betraying the faery cause and summoned
the Council to judge him. Rothlan was exiled for the
part he played and since then his lands have been
ringed by magic. It is here, in the hill that we hold the
set of fabulous firestones whose spell keeps the ring of
power round Jarishan."

"Jarishan?" queried Sir James.

"Rothlan's great estate. It was once a place of great
beauty but what it will be like now, I cannot tell. The
sun never shines there and his famous eagles, his mes-
sengers of the skies ... well, they were changed to trav-
esties of their former majesty. That I did not agree to,
as they had done their master's bidding and the fault
was not theirs, but Prince Kalman and the Lords of the
North were adamant and I was outvoted. So the eagles
became monstrous things, doomed to suffer with their
master. As for Alasdair Rothlan; well, he was cut off
completely from then on. I've never seen him since."

"But surely," Neil said doubtfully, "he must be hundreds of years old by now? And you ...?" he broke off in
embarrassment.

The MacArthur smiled. "By your time, I suppose, we
are really quite ancient," he admitted. "But we're faeries, you see. We don't age in the same way you do. Our
time is different from yours. Alasdair Rothlan is still
quite a young man."

"And this Amgarad?" queried Clara.

"Amgarad was the captain of his eagles. I knew him
well in the old days. A fine, proud bird."

"He isn't now," she remarked, remembering the foul
monster that had attacked them at the well. Her heart
softened in pity. "Poor Amgarad," she said sadly.

9. The Dragon's Lair

A few days after Sir James's memorable visit, a triumphant Dougal MacLeod also found his way into the hill. As he made his way down the steep tunnels, he was bursting with pride at his own cleverness. Convinced that Sir James was engaged in a mammoth plot to defraud Customs and Excise, he had had no difficulty at all in picking up the illicit pipeline with a metal-detector. Its steady clicking had led him straight to a slit-like opening on the lower slopes of the Park, not far from the distillery itself. Suddenly, he stopped and sniffed. The aroma was unmistakeable. Whisky! Good Scotch whisky!

"Whisky!" he said aloud. "My, oh my, Sir James, I've got you this time!"

Gleefully he followed the tunnel downwards until he came to a large cavern. By this time, the smell of whisky was overpowering. Moving forward he flashed his torch around the walls of the cave, which, had he but known it, was Arthur's lair.

Arthur, as it happened, was in an extremely bad temper. Since their visit to the hill, Sir James and Jamie Todd had been busy in the distillery and between them had managed to rig up a powerful pump that in a few days had reduced Arthur's wonderful lake to little more than a puddle. Bored and disgruntled, he lay (as dragon's do) on his bed of treasure and bemoaned his loss.

It so happened that the beam of the torch passed over Arthur as he reared his horned head to investigate the unaccustomed sound of the metal-detector. Dougal MacLeod froze in absolute horror as his brain registered the unbelieveable sight of a creature he had previously only seen in the décor of Chinese restaurants! Interestedly, Arthur watched as the beam of the torch stopped abruptly and then, gingerly, moved slowly back to light up not only Arthur, but also the magnificent treasure that he lay upon. Amid the glittering piles of gold plate, sovereigns and ornate crowns, sparkled rubies, sapphires, diamonds and emeralds but, more startling than any of them, were jewels that shone with a translucent amber brilliance that pierced Dougal to the heart.

Transfixed by the sprawling glory of the treasure, he was brought sharply back to reality as the dragon moved its sinuous body and bent its great head to investigate the intruder.

Gasping in horror at the sudden movement, Dougal involuntarily jerked his torch upwards, blinding Arthur with its glare. He reared in annoyance, spread his wings and gave a roar that shook the cavern, totally drowning out Dougal's scream of fear as he dropped his metal-detector and ran for his life.

It was much later that Hamish entered the MacArthur's Hall followed by a prisoner who shambled unwillingly after him. Hamish bowed before the MacArthur and gestured towards the bound man at his side.

"His name, he says, is Dougal MacLeod. I'm thinking that he's the man that keeps count of all the whisky in Sir James's wee factory outside."

The MacArthur looked disapproving. "I hope ye will not be referring to Sir James's grand distillery as a 'wee factory' in his hearing, Hamish. You know how proud he is of it. Now, where did you find this fellow?"

"In the tunnels, MacArthur. He must have found Arthur and got a bit of a fright, for we found this weapon in his cave where he dropped it." Archie stepped forward and waved the metal-detector at MacLeod, who cowered back.

"Who are you?" thundered the MacArthur. "You come here to threaten us! With weapons!"

"No, no," gabbled MacLeod frantically. "Nothing of the kind! I was only following a pipeline from the distillery. It led to a big cave with ... well, what looked like a dragon in it!"

"It was a dragon," confirmed the MacArthur. "*Our* dragon. Do you have any objection to our having a dragon?"

Hastily, MacLeod retracted. "No ... no," he said. "None in the world. It was just a wee bit unexpected, that's all."

"Unexpected! Un – ex – pect – ed!" He took the metal-detector from Archie's hands and waved it at Dougal MacLeod. "Do you expect me to believe that? You come here with this fearsome weapon to kill our dragon and then say it was unexpected!"

"But I didn't come here to kill your dragon," wailed Dougal.

By this time, the MacArthur had worked himself into a fine old rage. "You're all the same," he screeched. "All the same! All out to kill these poor, harmless, inoffensive creatures with your swords and your lances. Just so that you can go back home and boast of having killed a fierce dragon. Take him out of my sight, Hamish!" He gestured dismissively.

"But please ..." Dougal struggled violently as Hamish led him, none too gently, out of the Hall.

"Come, Archie," beckoned the MacArthur. "You know the Ranger's house. Go and tell him, or one of his children, what has happened. Ask him to tell Sir James that we have a prisoner in the hill and that his name is Dougal MacLeod."

10. Pigeon Post

At first glance, there was really nothing remarkable about them at all. Two ordinary-looking pigeons sitting on the windowsill of an Edinburgh school was not guaranteed to excite much interest in passers-by at the best of times, and it had to be admitted that this was hardly the best of times. The weather had again turned cold and the thick mist, known to Edinburgh residents as the "haar," had returned.

Cars and buses, their visibility now reduced to almost zero, picked their way tentatively up and down the narrow confines of the High Street and the hardy citizens of the Canongate were far too interested in finishing their shopping to worry about a couple of pigeons.

Had they been more attentive, however, they would have realized that the pigeons, on their lofty windowsill, seemed a strangely anxious pair. Their beady eyes missed nothing as the mist swirled coldly round the school playground. "I don't much like this haar, Jaikie," remarked one. "I think his lordship must have conjured it up!"

"Ocht! You've got his lordship on the brain, Archie!" replied Jaikie. "Ever since Clara told us about that bird that attacked them on the hill."

"Well, who else could it be but Amgarad? Feathers like dirty rags, Clara said." He shivered. "And Amgarad on the loose means that Rothlan isn't far away!"

"But why would he send a mist? Edinburgh weather is always changeable. It's often like this," Despite his words Jaikie was not as confident as he sounded and looking rather anxiously around, shrank a bit further back against the window.

"Aye. There's probably nothing in it. Just another haar," remarked Archie.

"As long as Amgarad isn't in it!" muttered Jaikie. "We're pigeons, remember!"

"Well, I didn't ask to be a pigeon!" retorted Archie huffily. "I wanted to be an eagle! This pigeon business is just a dead loss. Why couldn't we have been eagles instead of stupid pigeons? What a life! Nothing but cooo, cooo and peck, peck all the time. My feet are freezing!"

"Archie! Will ye haud yer whisht! An eagle! We're supposed to be unobtrusive, we're supposed to melt into the scenery and you — you want to be an eagle! For goodness sake, this is the High Street, not the Highlands! We're not here to cause a sensation and if it weren't for your stupidity, we wouldn't be here in the first place!"

"I ken! I ken, but I'm that cold and starving hungry. How long do they keep these children in the classrooms for anyway?"

Jaikie fluffed his feathers against the chill mist and shifted on his claws. "Don't ask me," he muttered, "but Hamish said we had to talk to Neil, so we'll just have to hang around until they let him into the playground."

Archie eyed him sulkily. "Let's do something then. What about taking a look through the windows to see if we can see him or Clara?"

Neil, as it happened, was not hard to find. The pigeons spotted him at the first window they looked through. The children in the class looked up as the birds fluttered against the glass.

"Look, Miss! Pigeons!"

"Yes," agreed the teacher, "and you have all seen pigeons before, so don't try to change the subject.

Now," she looked at the clock, "make a line by the door. It's time for play."

A short time later Neil followed the rest of his class downstairs, full of excitement at seeing the pigeons. They had never, ever, come to the school before. Something really important must have happened, he thought, for them to take such a risk.

The school janitor, Old MacGregor, stood dourly by the playground door. Neil saw him peering suspiciously into the mist amd hurried towards him. A thin, dirty-looking black and white cat seemed to be the object of his wrath. He stamped his foot at it threateningly as it tried to slink into the warmth.

"Shoo! Shoo!" he shouted at it, "go on, off with you!" The cat miaowed pathetically and backed off into the mist.

"Dinna you be feeding that cat," the janitor called after Neil as he went into the playground. "I've seen you encouraging it with bits of sandwich!"

"But it's a stray and it's starving, Mr MacGregor," Neil protested.

"I'm no' having it here! Now mind what I say or I'll be telling your dad on you!"

Neil grinned at him, knowing that the threat was an empty one, and slipped with the rest of his class into the swirling whiteness of the haar. He walked to one side and had barely taken the sandwich from his pocket when he felt the cat rubbing round his ankles. Kneeling down, he undid the plastic bag and broke the sandwich up for her. Poor thing, he thought, she was so thin and the summer holidays were near. Who was going to feed her then?

A burst of loud laughter told him that Graham Flint and his gang were nearby. The cat heard them too and alert to danger, disappeared before he could give her the other half of the sandwich. It was only when he looked round to call her that he realized how really thick the haar was. Fear gripped him for an instant as he remembered his last encounter in such weather. Quickly, he groped his way towards where he thought the school wall ought to be and sighed with relief when it loomed in front of him. Now that he had his bearings, he felt more confident. "Hamish!" he called quietly. "Hamish!"

There was a sudden flap of wings as two pigeons fluttered down to land on his shoulders.

"Hello, Neil," said one. "Hamish couldn't come. I'm Jaikie and that's Archie."

"I thought it was you when I saw you at the window. What's happened? Is anything wrong?"

"We've brought a message from the MacArthur for you to pass on to your father and Sir James. That man, Dougal MacLeod, he got into the hill and discovered Arthur!"

"Dougal MacLeod! In the hill?" Neil gasped at that particular piece of information. "Gosh! That's a disaster!" he muttered, horrified. Then he visualized the effect it would have on Sir James. "Good Lord!" he whispered, "Sir James will go absolutely mental! But what happened? Where is he now?"

"He's in the hill. We have him prisoner. The MacArthur wants to see Sir James urgently."

"I bet he does," said Neil feelingly, "but look, there's a problem. I'll not be able to leave school until half past three."

"That doesn't matter," said Jaikie, "as long as the message is passed on." He flexed his wings as if to fly off, but Archie had seen the sandwich in Neil's hand.

"Hey, we don't need to fly back just yet," he said, leaning forward and rubbing his head against Neil's cheek.

"Don't tell me, Archie," grinned Neil. "You're starving hungry as usual, am I right?"

"I really am, Neil, and your mother makes grand sandwiches!" cooed Archie.

Neil held up his sandwich as Archie and then Jaikie hopped down his sleeve and started to peck at it hungrily. They were still pecking away happily when Graham Flint and his cronies appeared suddenly.

"Here he is!" said Graham Flint triumphantly. "Will you just look at him! He's feeding the pigeons now! At least it's a change from that manky old cat!"

There was a burst of laughter as they crowded nearer. Jaikie and Archie fluttered into the air in alarm as the boys came closer but they had their own built-in means of retaliation. As they flew over Graham Flint, they dropped two rather large calling cards — and despite the mist, their aim was true.

As Graham clawed the white muck from his hair, the pigeons soared above the school. "If only we had both been eagles," was Archie's regretful remark as they flew back towards the hill.

11. Plots and Plans

That evening, Sir James, the Ranger, Jamie Todd and the children sat grouped around the MacArthur's throne in the Great Hall.

"The thing is," Sir James was saying, "you can't keep him here indefinitely. He's a senior officer and is bound to have told someone where he was going."

"In other words," confirmed Jamie, "if you're not careful, you'll have a visit from Customs and Excise. And not a social call either."

The MacArthur heaved a sigh. "We can't have that!"

Clara looked shyly at Sir James. "But if you let him go, won't he tell the Excise people what he found and bring them straight here?"

Neil looked at her in disgust. "Use your head, Clara," he said. "If he tells them about Arthur, they'll think he's gone completely off his rocker."

"But don't you see, Neil? He doesn't need to tell them anything about Arthur. He just has to get them outside the distillery with metal-detectors and the pipe-line will lead them straight here!"

"You leave that side of it to me," interrupted the MacArthur. "We have ways of protecting ourselves. The main problem was stopping Arthur's supply and that has been done."

"How is Arthur taking it now that there is no more whisky?" asked Jamie.

The MacArthur heaved a sigh. "It was bad enough when he noticed that his lake was shrinking but when it disappeared altogether he went wild. Roared around slurping up all the wee pools he could find and then rampaged about blowing fire and smoke everywhere. I've had my fill of that dragon, I can tell you!"

"But he seems quite resigned now, does he?"

The MacArthur grinned. "Well, according to Archie, he still hangs hopefully around the tap but I think he'll be all right as long as no one," and here he glared at Archie, "gives him any more whisky."

"Och! I'll no' be doing that again in a hurry, MacArthur. It's just that Arthur is more depressed than ever now."

Clara sounded sympathetic. "Is there nothing else that would cheer him up, Archie?" she asked.

"I ken fine what would cheer him up but it's a pretty impossible dream."

"Tell us anyway," asked Clara.

"Well, he's always talking about his lady-love. A beautiful dragon she was, but after the troubles he doesn't even know if she survived. Bessie, her name was."

"Bessie!" she repeated thoughtfully," her head tilting to one side. Then her eyes sharpened. "Archie, did you say ... Bessie?"

"Aye."

"Now think carefully, Archie. Did Arthur ever call her ... Nessie?"

"Now that you mention it, I believe he did."

"My ... Goodness!!!" whispered Sir James.

"The Loch Ness ... Clara! Do you realize what you're saying?" gasped her brother.

The MacArthur, at a loss to know what was happening but aware that he had missed something vital along the line, gave a thunderous roar. "Will – You – Tell – Me – What – You – Are – All – Talking – About?" he screeched.

Clara said excitedly. "You see, MacArthur, we think we know who Arthur's Nessie is! Wouldn't it be great if we could bring them together again after all these years? Then Arthur wouldn't be lonely any more."

The MacArthur looked as though he were about to burst a blood vessel. "I am *not*," he stated, "I am *not* going to have another dragon in this hill! One is quite enough! Two would be two too many! I won't have it, I tell you! I am not giving a home to any more dragons and that's flat!"

"But I wasn't thinking of bringing Nessie here," explained Clara, her eyes alight. "I was thinking of taking Arthur to Nessie!"

Sir James almost had a fit. "Are you quite out of your mind, Clara? How on earth do you suppose that we could get a dragon from one side of Scotland to the other without anyone noticing? On a lead?" He threw out his hands helplessly. "Dragons, may I remind you, aren't exactly everyday objects, you know. It would be bad enough transporting an elephant. People at least know what elephants are. But a dragon?" He shook his head. "It's quite impossible!"

The MacArthur coughed. "Where," he asked, "where does this other dragon live?"

"Up in the Highlands," answered Neil. "They called a loch after her, Loch Ness."

"Humph," grunted the MacArthur, "did they now. Nothing new in that! Why do you think this hill is called Arthur's Seat, eh?"

"The Highlands," Archie crooned. "My, I'd love to see the mountains again."

"We are not going to the Highlands, with or without a dragon, and that's final!" snorted Sir James.

The MacArthur drew himself up to his full height, which wasn't very high, and said authoritatively, "I am in favour of it!"

"You would be," said Sir James, "but ..."

"I am, too," announced Jamie Todd. He quailed at the withering glare that Sir James shot at him but continued bravely. "Well, I am, Sir James. This here dragon has been nothing but a pack of trouble for as long as I can remember. If we can get rid of him for good then I think we should take the chance!"

"Well spoken," said the MacArthur, slapping his knee. "My sentiments entirely!"

Sir James looked stunned. "You're in favour of it? You must be out of your minds. All of you! Even if we did manage to get a vehicle big enough to carry him, what on earth would we do when we got to the shores of Loch Ness? Whole expeditions with the latest equipment spend months patrolling Loch Ness, hoping for a glimpse of her! What would we do? Stand at the edge of the water like complete ninnies shouting 'Nessie! Nessie!'"

"Och! I can solve that problem," said the MacArthur. "If Arthur's Nessie is in that loch then there will be faeries looking after her. Dragons can't fend for themselves at all. Actually, my daughter, Ellan, is visiting the Highlands at the moment and I will have her make all the arrangements." He broke off in annoyance. "Weel, Hamish? What is it?"

A worried-looking Hamish, who had been trying to get a word in edgeways, now bowed low before his master. "MacArthur," he said anxiously, "please give the matter some thought. Is it wise to let Arthur go?"

The MacArthur had the grace to look uncomfortable but stuck firmly to his guns. "I'm fed up with that confounded dragon, Hamish!" he growled. "Completely fed up! And I don't see what difference it will make if he goes or stays. As long as we have the firestones, we are perfectly safe. We don't need Arthur!"

Wishing fervently that the MacArthur's daughter, the Lady Ellan, had not chosen that particular time to visit her mother's family in the Highlands, Hamish persisted in his argument.

"Nevertheless, MacArthur, I don't think it's a good idea for Arthur to leave us. It's too risky now that Amgarad has been seen on the hill. Lady Ellan would be the first to tell you so! Master," he sounded anguished, "there are too many questions that remain unanswered! How did Amgarad break out of Jarishan? Why is he here? Is Lord Rothlan's power returning? I beg you; please keep Arthur here in the hill. This has been his home for hundreds of years. I'm sure Lady Ellan would agree."

But the MacArthur, annoyed perhaps at the implication that his daughter knew better than he did, was adamant. "If we can get Arthur to Loch Ness," he said flatly, "then he's going! And if it will make you any happier then you can take the firestones into your care the minute Arthur leaves the hill! But he is going, Hamish." He put his hand on the top of his head. "I've had that dragon up to here!"

The Ranger then chipped in. "Actually, I think I can solve the transport problem," he said. "A farmer friend of mine often grazes his sheep on the hill. He'll be bringing a flock down tomorrow and he owes me a few favours. There'll be no problem about us having the use of his transporter for a few days. It's a massive thing!"

"Hang on a bit, Dad," interrupted Neil. "Before we make any plans, hadn't we better tell Arthur? After all, he might not like being shut up in a big lorry and bumped over half of Scotland!"

"Don't you worry about Arthur!" said the MacArthur grimly. "He's going whether he likes it or not. Did you say that the transporter will be free tomorrow, Ranger?"

"Aye! Tomorrow afternoon."

"Then," said the MacArthur, "if everybody is in agreement, I suggest we plan 'Operation Arthur' for tomorrow night!"

12. Operation Arthur

It was a dark night, for which Sir James was profoundly thankful. As he and the Ranger stood beside the enormous transporter, waiting for Arthur to appear, Sir James shifted impatiently on his feet. "I wish they'd get a move on," he muttered, looking round.

The Ranger too surveyed the scene with some misgiving, for the side of the hill was more than a trifle crowded. Apart from the flock of sheep that had been off-loaded from the transporter, the slopes were also home to a mass of MacArthurs who were being regimented here and there by their agitated chief.

He eyed the proceedings apprehensively. "I don't like the look of this," he said to the Ranger. "It's busier than Piccadilly Circus up here! What on earth is the MacArthur up to?"

The Ranger swept an eye over the ranks of the MacArthurs. "I don't know," he said slowly. "You'd almost think he was expecting trouble!"

Sir James muttered something under his breath.

The Ranger's lips twisted in a smile. "How is everything going at the distillery?" he asked in an attempt to divert Sir James's mind from the anxieties of the present.

Sir James's face brightened. "Jamie," he answered, sounding considerably more cheerful, "is just finishing things off for me. He's done a wonderful job. We've managed to retrieve most of the whisky; so much so that I doubt if anyone will be able to tell that there was ever any discrepancy."

"Pity he'll miss seeing the dragon, though," remarked the Ranger.

Clara rushed over to them, brimming with excitement. "Arthur's coming now, Dad. And he's really something. Look ... there he is now!"

The dragon emerged from the tunnel, his brilliant colours caught in the light of the MacArthurs' torches. They watched as he moved forward across the hillside, flexing his wings in joy at being above ground. As he felt the breath of the cool night air, the dragon lifted his great head, stretched his powerful wings and flapped them experimentally.

"Dear goodness," gasped Sir James in horror, "he's ... he's going to fly!"

The MacArthurs, to give them their due, did what they could. They made a concerted rush for Arthur, but against a dragon they had their limits. The night air, the starry sky and the limitless curve of the heavens had woken old memories in Arthur. With a few effortless flaps of his wings he left the earth behind and soared skywards, revelling in his new-found freedom.

The MacArthur stomped up to the transporter looking sour.

"What are we going to do now," gasped Sir James in a panic.

"I wouldn't worry, Sir James. He'll no be gone long, more's the pity. Look over yonder!"

Neil grabbed Sir James's arm. "Look over there! An aeroplane!"

"Oh no! It's the London Shuttle!"

"I'd love to see the pilot's face when he sees Arthur," said Neil, watching with fascinated eyes as Arthur soared towards the plane.

The pilot of the Shuttle picked Arthur up in the powerful beam of his landing lights and at first refused to believe his eyes. His first incredulous thought was that Arthur was a kite or even a stray balloon but the steadily beating wings and supple movement of his body soon banished that idea from his mind. This was a living, flying dragon straight from the pages of a storybook.

"What the devil?" he said savagely to his co-pilot as he banked hard to avoid colliding with Arthur. His co-pilot, in much the same state of disbelief, shook his head in amazement. "A dragon! But ... but, they don't exist ... do they?"

"This one looks pretty solid to me!" muttered the pilot grimly as he banked again.

Dragons, as one would expect, do not rate highly in any of the emergency procedures that pilots routinely follow. The Air Traffic Controller at Edinburgh Airport, enquiring politely as to why flight B6672 had left its flight-path to career wildly across his radar screen was not amused to be told by the pilot that he was trying to avoid a dragon, especially when the blips on his radar screen showed nothing of the sort.

"I don't care if you're not picking anything else up," snarled the pilot, craning his neck to see where Arthur had gone. "Why don't you just look out of your window?"

Against the backdrop of the night sky the Air Traffic controller saw the shape of the dragon, and watched in horror as Arthur flapped interestedly around the Shuttle.

Clara watched in dismay as the pilot put his aircraft into a steep climb. As it soared upwards, the resultant turbulence hit Arthur full on and sent him tumbling head over tail in a wild spin that left him disoriented and dizzy. Watching the performance in the sky, the MacArthur shouted triumphantly and ran towards the transporter. "Get the ramp down, Ranger, and be ready for him!"

"You mean he'll come back?" asked Sir James.

"The daft beast! Of course he'll come back! All he's ever met in the sky before are golden eagles. That plane has probably scared the wits oot o' him." The MacArthur grabbed Neil's torch and started to wave it wildly. "Come here, Arthur," he roared in a mighty voice. "Come here, ye great daft thing!"

"There he is," shouted the Ranger. "He's coming in low."

The plane's surge of power and dreadful roar had reduced Arthur to a shivering bag of nerves. Now totally petrified, he headed like an arrow for home. The MacArthurs saw him coming and scattered for their lives as he came in low, hit the ground at speed and ended up in a tangle of legs and wings, not far from the transporter.

From his perch, high up on the crags, Amgarad looked on with interest and some sympathy. These new monsters of the skies seemed beyond even the power of dragons! And only a few yards from Sir James, Dougal MacLeod also watched the proceedings with interest. In the general excitement, he had managed to free himself and revenge burned deep within him as he watched everyone dashing towards the dragon.

"Get Arthur over here, quickly!" Sir James shouted anxiously. "There's bound to be trouble!"

"Trouble?" Neil asked.

"The police, Neil! They're bound to have contacted them. They'll be here any minute, I should imagine. Look, you and Clara had better get into the cab of the transporter. Once we get Arthur inside, we won't be hanging around!"

Arthur, still in a state of shock and frantically trying to hide his head under his wings, was refusing to move.

The MacArthur went over to him and gave him a great buffet with his arm.

"Come on, Arthur! Get moving! Up the ramp with you! Remember, you're on your way to see your Nessie and we're all coming with you," he said determinedly.

Arthur opened a wonderful eye that was quite unlike any other eye that Sir James had ever seen. It blinked resignedly as he heaved himself grudgingly to his feet and obediently clawed his way up the ramp into the gaping maw of the transporter.

"In with you all!" screamed the MacArthur. In an instant the MacArthurs ran to the flock of sheep being held beside the transporter and, to Sir James's amazement, seemed to dissolve into them. Watching from behind the rocks, Dougal MacLeod, too, watched with incredulous eyes. The MacArthurs seemed to have melted into the sheep, who now seemed to be sheep with a mission! As one, the flock moved purposefully towards the transporter and, in minutes, had pushed and scrambled its way up the ramp to join Arthur.

When the last sheep was bundled in, Sir James and the MacArthur hastily raised the ramp and fastened the metal pegs that held the back doors in place before running to the front of the enormous vehicle and climbing hurriedly into the cab. The Ranger started the engine and, with a clashing of gears, the huge transporter lurched forward. Slowly and carefully it moved down the slope and set off for the distant shores of Loch Ness.

13. Firestones

Dougal MacLeod, however, did not wait to see it leave and did not care where it was going. Whilst everyone's attention had been concentrated on the dragon, his mind pictured an empty cave and unguarded treasure. Indeed, the memory of the wonderful jewels in Arthur's cave had haunted him ever since he had first seen them. Now that the dragon had left the hill, and most of the MacArthurs with him, it seemed an ideal opportunity to return to the cave to take one more look at the fabulous stones.

Although he told himself that he merely wanted to see them again, Dougal knew in his heart that he really meant to take them. In truth, he was powerless to think otherwise since the fault lay in the stones themselves, for they were magic stones and it was their power that drew Dougal helplessly to them.

He was careful to enter the hill from the entrance that he had discovered on the lower slopes and it did not take him long to reach the entrance to Arthur's cave. He shone a torch round its high walls and then, confident that he was alone, illuminated the treasure itself. Lying as Arthur had left it, it lay strewn untidily across the floor of the cave in scattered heaps that glittered and sparkled in the torchlight.

The fiery amber stones drew Dougal like a magnet. Uncaringly, he scrunched and slipped over gold and priceless jewels to reach the pieces that held the stones. Kneeling on top of a mound of treasure, his eyes shone as he held up a delicate belt of gold filigree studded with stones the size of sovereigns, a fabulous ring and a most beautiful necklace, all of which glowed with the mysterious and irresistible amber fire.

Something made him look into the darkness and conscious that he had been in the cave for some time, he hurriedly tied the wonderful jewels in his handkerchief and made to leave. He shivered. The darkness that surrounded him had become strangely oppressive and, although it might have been his imagination, he thought that he heard a slight sound.

Flashing his torch for reassurance, the beam instead revealed the terrible sight of Amgarad swooping towards him, eyes blazing, wings wide and talons outstretched. Dougal froze in horror, but only for a second. Instinctively, he threw the heavy torch at Amgarad. It was, as it happened, a lucky throw. The torch hit Amgarad on the side of his head and knocked him to the ground in a swirling heap of feathers. Dougal did not wait. Feeling for the handkerchief, he picked up the bundle of jewels, stuffed them into his pocket and took off into the blackness. In his panic, however, he missed the entrance to the tunnel and ran straight into the wall of the cave.

The pain of the collision brought him to his senses and, cowering against the wall, he took stock of a situation that suddenly seemed full of unknown horrors. Where had that dreadful bird come from and were there any others perched in the cave, ready to strike? Looking back, he saw Amgarad's body lying in the torchlight, but nothing else moved. Still shaking with shock he crept towards the still, monstrous body of the bird and, grabbing his torch, shone it frantically round until its beam revealed the black entrance to the tunnel. All he could think of was escape, and making for the tunnel, he stumbled like a madman up its steep incline until, panting with exhaustion, he saw the starry glimmer of the night sky and knew he was safe.

He stepped out onto the hill, then stopped abruptly and gazed around in amazement. The park resembled a disaster zone. There were policemen everywhere! Helicopters flew overhead and police cars, lights flashing and sirens wailing, sped round the network of roads that lace the park.

"Good grief!" he muttered. "What on earth!" Then it clicked. The dragon! They were looking for Arthur!

Looking like a tramp after his ordeal and conscious of the bundle of jewels in his pocket, Dougal did not think it wise to move into the open. Instead, he hid inside the tunnel, wondering what on earth he was going to do. Two police cars, blue lights flashing, were parked nearby and it was obvious that anyone found loitering on the hill at this hour would be taken to the nearest police station for questioning. Dougal groaned and cursed the dragon.

He remained crouched inside the tunnel for the best part of the night and although the policemen came worryingly close, the entrance to the tunnel was well hidden. It was almost dawn before the two police cars moved off to circle the park.

It was this factor, plus some worrying noises from the inside of the tunnel, that tempted Dougal to move out onto the hill. It certainly saved him from another encounter with Amgarad who, having recovered from the stunning blow, had been creeping stealthily towards him. Although still dazed, Amgarad was determined to fight to get the firestones back.

He was a minute too late, however, as a frightened Dougal, hearing him approach, slipped quietly out onto the hill. Amgarad, seeing his quarry escape, frantically flapped to the entrance but had to watch in helpless fury as Dougal made his way towards the shelter of a rocky outcrop. It was not only Amgarad, however, who saw the creeping figure. A burly policeman, stationed on the slopes above, also saw Dougal moving towards the rocks. Reacting swiftly, he leapt down the incline and threw his arms around the shadowy figure.

"Got you, my lad!" he said. His arms, however, clasped empty air and although the policeman could have sworn that he had actually grabbed someone, his senses told him otherwise. The person had disappeared! He looked round and could see no one.

Dougal, too, could not understand what had happened to him. He had felt the policeman's arms grip him and had heard his voice ... and then nothing! He was standing on his own by the rock. He looked around but, to his astonishment, the policeman seemed to have disappeared! His relief, however, was short-lived for, as he peered into the darkness, two other policemen ran up.

"What's up, Ian? Did you get him?"

"I ... I could have sworn I saw someone but ... it must have been the rocks casting a shadow." The policeman peered around. "There's no one here! Sorry, chaps."

It was at that particular moment that Dougal freaked! The two policemen seemed to be talking to him and he could see them quite plainly but it was also obvious that they could not see him! He walked back up the slope and, to his horror, the legs that moved were not his own! It was then that he remembered that the MacArthurs had merged into the flock of sheep before climbing into the transporter. Had he somehow merged with the policeman? The thought terrified him! But how had it happened? He kept very still and looked out of the policeman's eyes at the darkness of the hill. He wondered if the policeman could read his thoughts and if he knew that he, Dougal MacLeod, was sharing his body.

"This is awful!" thought Dougal wildly. "What if I can't get out again!"

The policeman, however, seemed unaware of anything amiss and as he calmly continued to patrol the hillside, Dougal gradually relaxed at the very ordinariness of the occupation.

"I wonder," he thought, "if I can use him to get me out of this mess. The High Street isn't far. If only I could get through the cordon!" Dougal concentrated his mind on leaving the hill and, to his relief, the policeman started to make his way down the slope towards the road.

No one but Amgarad seemed to notice that the policeman had left the hill and was walking towards the police cars, fire engines and ambulances that sealed off the park from the public. Still dizzy, Amgarad shook his head, stretched his wings and flew unnoticed to the houses at the foot of the High Street, determined to follow the firestones to their destination.

Dougal, feeling much more confident, strode through the barrier knowing that no one would stop him. Once through the cordon, however, he guided the policeman's steps to a narrow passageway at the foot of the High Street.

"Now," he thought, "now I have to try to escape!"

He gathered himself and his mind together and stepped out of the policeman's body. He had succeeded! He felt faint with relief as he looked down and saw his own dusty trousers and scuffed shoes. He held his breath and stood very still as the policeman gave himself a slight shake, looked alertly up and down the High Street and then, realizing that he was supposed to be part of the action round the barricade, moved back towards the police cordon.

The relief was enormous! Dougal felt washed out and exhausted but, as he moved out into the High Street and turned his feet for home, he remembered the fabulous jewels that he carried. As he slipped his hand into his pocket to feel their reassuring bulk, a sense of triumph and power surged through him.

He would not, however, have felt quite so happy had he known that Amgarad, watching from the rooftops, was following him home.

14. The Loch Ness Monster

As Dougal MacLeod strode the streets of Edinburgh, Neil and Clara climbed down from the cab of the transporter, stretched their cramped legs and looked over the blue waters of Loch Ness.

"Here at last," laughed Clara delightedly, as she breathed in the wet smell of the loch that gleamed before them in the morning sun. Little ripples splashed on a narrow bank of pebbles where tree branches hung limply over the water.

"What do you think then, MacArthur?" queried Sir James. "The bank here is a bit steep but if we drive much further on we'll find ourselves too exposed for comfort. And we are on a bend, as you asked."

"Aye. The place is fine." He scanned the road in both directions and saw that it was clear. "Let's get the sheep out of the back of the transporter while the going's good." They moved to the back of the vehicle where the Ranger was already unfastening the pegs and preparing to let down the ramp.

"I hate to dash your hopes," said Sir James looking keenly over the loch, "but there isn't any sign of Nessie."

"Have patience, Sir James. She'll be out there somewhere, never fear. Just let's get things organized here first. We don't want any passing motorist to see Arthur, do we?"

"No, no, certainly not."

"I told the Ranger to park on the bend so that I could put the sheep on either side of the transporter. If any motorists do come along then we can easily hold the traffic up while Arthur gets out."

Sir James laughed. "A brilliant idea!" he announced. "Let's get started."

As the ramp was lowered, the sheep streamed out purposefully in both directions and proceeded to mill about aimlessly in the middle of the road. Sir James regarded them with approval. Certainly, with them in place, no car coming from either direction would be able to see what was going on by the side of the loch.

The transporter, now empty of sheep, revealed Arthur in all his glory. He was a magnificent dragon, red scales glistened over his sinuous body, his head was fearsome and horned and his fleshy wings were webbed in glittering gold. Archie was the only MacArthur left inside and was in a dreadful state, clutching an edge of Arthur's wing in one hand and scrubbing tears out of his eyes with the other.

"Arthur! Arthur! How can I leave you?" He started to cry bitterly and for a moment the dragon lowered his great head and rubbed his cheek on Archie's tattered sheepskin jacket, to give him comfort.

"Come on then, Arthur. It's time to go," Archie sobbed. They left the transporter together and, as Arthur clawed his ungainly way across the grey tarmac road to the edge of the loch, a small, slim woman ran down the hillside towards them.

"Father!" she called. "Father! I'm here!"

"Ellan!"

She slipped gracefully through the bushes and ran to hug her father. It showed in every line of his face that the MacArthur thought the world of his daughter and he proudly introduced her to Sir James and the Ranger. Clara and Neil came up from the shores of the loch and took an instant liking to the beautiful,

fair-haired young woman, who seemed to glow with
youth and laughter.

"Well," she said to her father, "I see you have brought
Arthur to Loch Ness as you promised."

"I have," he said, albeit a trifle defensively.

She regarded him steadily and shrugged slightly.
"What is done, is done. Let's hope that no trouble
comes from it."

"Whatever comes from it will be nothing like the
trouble we've already had," snorted the MacArthur.

They moved down to the loch side and Arthur
showed his happiness at seeing Lady Ellan by kneeling
awkwardly in front of her and bending his head to the
ground.

"Arthur!" she chided gently. "What is this that I have
been hearing? Setting the hill ablaze with your fire?"

Arthur looked more than upset; he looked a thor-
oughly mortified dragon. As Clara watched, he covered
his head with his wings in shame. Large tears welled
from his eyes and spilled down his cheeks. They were
no ordinary tears, however, for as they splashed to
the ground, the strangest thing happened. The tears
solidified into glowing jewels that shone with a piercing
amber light that Dougal MacLeod would have recog-
nised immediately.

"How gorgeous!" Clara exclaimed, picking them up
and holding them out to Lady Ellan. "Arthur's tears
have turned into beautiful jewels!"

Lady Ellan held them in her hand and looked at
Arthur. "They are very rare and very precious," she
said softly. "Dear Arthur, don't cry. Truly there is no
need. My father and I hope you will be very happy here
in Loch Ness and if you are not, you know we will be
more than happy to have you back in the hill." She cast
her father a warning glance as she said this and with

an effort he bit back the words that had sprung to his lips.

"Now, Arthur, you will really have to stop crying, you know, for I see your Nessie swimming through the loch towards us."

Arthur removed his wings from his face and reassured by her smiling words, scrambled to his feet and turned to face the loch. Lady Ellan walked with him to the water's edge where the waves were no longer gentle ripples but surges of brown water that crashed along the shore. Nessie had arrived!

Clara cringed back against Neil as the enormous creature heaved its massive bulk out of the water just feet from where she stood. Arthur held no fear for her but this dragon was very different and much bigger than Arthur. Her scaly hide, dripping with water and weeds, was dark grey with tinges of livid green, and her face had a speculative, hungry look that gave them all pause for thought. Indeed, Sir James made a quick calculation as to how quickly they could reach the safety of the transporter should things get out of hand.

Arthur, however, seemed to have no reservations and pushed forward waving his wings and hissing loudly with pleasure. The MacArthur and Lady Ellan raised their hands in salute as they moved away from the bank, but Archie ran crying into the waves shouting, "Goodbye, dear Arthur! Don't forget me!"

Perhaps Arthur didn't hear his cry for the noise of the wind or the slap of the waves but he didn't turn round to bid Archie farewell and it was Clara who stepped forward to hug him when he collapsed sobbing on the bank and Neil who helped mop up his tears.

They stood silently at the edge of the loch as the two great beasts swam into deep water and disappeared from view without a backward glance. Archie continued to give great hiccupping sobs and it was Clara who voiced all their thoughts. "I hope we've done the right thing bringing Arthur here. I didn't much like his Nessie!"

Lady Ellan, too, looked dubious but before she could answer, the hooting of a car horn and the frantic baaing of sheep brought them sharply back to the present and put all thoughts of Nessie from their minds.

"A car," snapped Sir James, looking up at the road. Hurriedly they scrambled up the bank to where an irate motorist was making little headway against a flock of sheep that had hemmed him in at the side of the road. Neil and Clara ducked down and ran for the safety of the cab followed by Sir James, the MacArthur and Lady Ellan and it was only when the door of the cab slammed shut that the Ranger moved forward to calm the situation and shepherd the sheep back into the transporter.

"Thank goodness that's over," Sir James confided to the Ranger as they left Loch Ness behind. "I hope I never have to live through another week like that. I couldn't stand the strain."

It was mid-afternoon by the time they reached Edinburgh. The bulk of the police contingent had long since left the park but when the transporter dropped Sir James at the distillery, his foreman was full of the events of the previous night.

"I knew the police were there," nodded Sir James, sipping a welcome cup of coffee. "They actually stopped the transporter last night as we left the park and made the Ranger open up the back."

"Did they no' see the dragon, then?" gasped Jamie.

Sir James grinned. "It was a bad moment," he admitted. "At the time I really thought we were all for the chop but I think the MacArthur must have cast a spell or something, because all the policemen saw in the back of the transporter were sheep. No Arthur, nothing; just a load of sheep."

"And what happened when you reached Loch Ness? Did you get rid of Arthur as planned?" queried Jamie.

"We did indeed! You know, Jamie, I can hardly believe that it all went so well. There were a thousand things that could have gone wrong but in the end it went without a hitch. The MacArthur was as good as his word. His daughter was there, you know, Lady Ellan! Now, she is my idea of a faery; such a beautiful girl. She had Nessie waiting for us, as arranged! And, do you know, we actually saw Nessie up close! A fearsome beast; not at all like Arthur. Anyway, they are together now and with any luck all our troubles are over!"

Sir James looked so cheerful that Jamie hardly knew how to break the bad news. "Er ... not quite, Sir James, not quite."

"What on earth do you mean?" Sir James looked startled. "We haven't lost any more whisky, have we?"

"Och, no! That's all taken care of! No, I'm talking about Dougal MacLeod! He got out of the hill while you were away."

"Dougal MacLeod!" echoed Sir James. "Do you know, I'd forgotten all about him! Thank heavens we managed to retrieve all that whisky, that's all I can say!" He looked sharply at Jamie. "You don't think that he'll be able to pin anything on us, do you?"

"It's nothing to do with the distillery, Sir James," reassured Jamie. "It's just that I had Hamish and Jaikie here this morning." He paused, shaking his head. "Gave me the fright of my life, it did, when two pigeons started talking to me in the yard! Frantic with worry they were! Seems that some treasure was stolen from the hill last night; those firestones that the MacArthur told us about. Hamish was going on about them something dreadful! He says it's all his fault!"

"The firestones? But who would take them from the hill?"

Jamie shrugged. "They didn't say, but MacLeod seems the obvious candidate. Anyway, they want you to help them and," he looked at his watch, "they'll be here soon to take you into the hill. There are still some police patrolling the slopes and they don't want you to be seen."

Sir James put his coffee cup down on the table, looking appalled.

"You must be joking!" he exclaimed in horror. "My part in all this has finished! *I've* got my whisky back and *they've* got rid of their dragon! End of story!"

"I'm sorry, sir," Jamie said worriedly, "but that's what they said!"

15. Summer in Jarishan

Lord Rothlan woke that morning to thunderous knocking on his bedroom door. He sat up abruptly in his massive four-poster bed, rubbed the sleep from his eyes and wondered what on earth was going on. Muttering under his breath, he wrapped a thick woollen plaid round his shoulders before pulling back one of the heavy draperies that surrounded his bed.

The great, carved door burst open as half of his household crowded into the room and watched as he stepped in sudden wonder from his bed. The room was transformed. Sunlight streamed in through the three tall windows that faced the east; it glowed in shining, golden bars on the ruby-red Persian carpets that scattered the floor and picked out the delicate gold and rose tones of the tapestries lining the walls. With a cry of delight, he ran to stand in its warmth, throwing his hands into the air in joy as his servants tumbled round him, laughing and clapping. Gathering the trailing plaid around him, he walked to one of the windows and looked out over the loch. The foul mist had disappeared and below him the waters of Loch Jarishan sparkled in the sunlight while, cavorting gaily in the air, his eagles soared high over the mountains in a sky of cloudless blue.

"The crystal!" he suddenly said aloud, as he realized the enormity of what must have happened for the magic shield to be lifted from his lands. "I must see the crystal!"

The castle was seized by madness as everyone rushed outside and luxuriated in the heavenly warmth of the sun. Summer had returned to Jarishan!

Trembling with excitement, Lord Rothlan held the crystal in both hands and again felt power surge through him as he watched the shadows take shape. The globe was glowing brightly and he caught his breath as many pictures started to unfold in its depths. He saw the MacArthur with his daughter beside him and his eyes dwelt for some time on Lady Ellan before the mists swirled and, to his relief, Amgarad appeared looking, it must be admitted, very much the worse for wear. His feathers seemed decidedly more ragged than usual and an ugly red swelling disfigured one side of his face. Perched unhappily on a spur of rock, his misery smote his master like a sword.

Rothlan concentrated his mind and spoke the words of an old spell, watching with dark, eager eyes to see if the enchantment still worked. Triumph surged through him as a faint beam of light lit Amgarad. He saw the bird's head lift suddenly and his eyes become alert and watchful. Contact had been made!

"Amgarad," said Lord Rothlan, staring feverishly into the glass. "Can you hear me?"

"I can hear you, Master!" replied Amgarad, flapping his wings.

"Tell me, Amgarad! Tell me quickly! What has happened?"

Amgarad poured out the story of his journey, the dragon and his adventures in the hill but started to stumble as he had to admit that in trying to steal the firestones, he had been worsted.

"Master, I was so close to them! I saw him hold them up! There was a belt, a necklace and a ring, all studded with firestones! Fabulous pieces! He wrapped them in a cloth and was about to take them away when I swooped on him out of the dark. But he must have heard the noise of my wings for he threw a heavy magic instrument at me. It knocked me out of the air and left me stunned and when I woke he had gone and the firestones with him. An army of humans is looking for him now on the slopes of the hill and the MacArthurs too are searching everywhere. They will not find him, though, for the thief escaped."

"Did you follow him, Amgarad? Do you know where he went?"

"I followed him, Master. I know where he lives."

"You have done well, my brave eagle! Your words explain many things! I believe the MacArthur has lost much of his power now that the firestones have left the hill. There can be no other reason for what has happened here!"

"Something has happened at Jarishan, Master?"

"A most wonderful thing, Amgarad! This morning when we woke, the sun was shining on Jarishan! It is summer! The lake is clear and your eagles are flying in the sunlight!"

"Master! I can hardly believe it! It must mean that it was the firestones that ..."

"... kept us captive," finished Lord Rothlan nodding, "I can think of no other explanation. It was only when they were taken out of the hill that the ring of magic round Jarishan was broken. The Council must have given them to the MacArthurs for safe-keeping. Interesting, isn't it, that they would not trust Prince Kalman with such power, and the firestones must have enormous power if they held the ring of magic round Jarishan! Amgarad, we must get them back from this thief before the MacArthur finds out where they are! They must never return to the hill! Now that the sun has returned to our lands I am determined that it will stay. Listen carefully! If the ring of magic that surrounds us really has disappeared then we will join you on the hill as soon as we can. I have many old scores to settle with the MacArthur and," he smiled unpleasantly, "I shall show him no mercy! We shall be with you soon, Amgarad!"

Lord Rothlan released the crystal ball from the grip of his fingers and watched as it misted over. "Call my captains," he told his valet as he stalked to the stairs, "we have much to discuss!"

That evening as Lord Rothlan and his captains surveyed their army as it marched, in kilted splendour, across the glen, Prince Kalman also watched with an anxious frown, from the shelter of a stand of trees on the hillside. He, too, had been amazed when the sun had suddenly bathed Jarishan in light and warmth that morning and now, with the snow melting all around him and flowers springing from the wet earth, he felt a surge of unease in the knowledge that the magic shield round Jarishan must have disappeared completely. And now this! An army marching for the border! But who on earth was Rothlan going to fight?

"Where *can* Rothlan be going with an army like that?" he pondered aloud.

Kitor clicked his beak non-committally. "Does it matter, Master? With Rothlan gone, the loch will be open to us, for only servants and the women and children are left. The water goblins are doing their best, but it's a huge loch. They need time!"

Kalman pressed his lips together in a thin line. "The crown *is* here!" he muttered. "I know it's here. I can feel its presence. That mad, old woman told me the truth!"

"She was too afraid not to, Master," the crow said dryly.

"She said it landed here and that my father's last spell bound it to the Meridens for ever. But why is it not revealing itself to me? Why?" Frustration laced the prince's voice as he watched the last remnants of Rothlan's army disappear into the hills. "Come Kitor; we'll leave Rothlan to his battles," he snapped. "Summon the water goblins to the boathouse! They must be told to work harder. We might not have much time left here and the crown must be found!"

As Rothlan's men marched over the sheep paths that led to the border, their spirits ran high. Rothlan, however, was more than a little worried. Spells were tricky things but he could think of no other way to move his army across Scotland unseen.

Topping a hill, they looked down on the waters of the broad river that rushed and tumbled swiftly among the rocks of a deep gorge. This was the boundary of Rothlan's domain and was regarded with both hope and some trepidation for they all knew that if they could cross the river, the spell that hemmed Jarishan in from the outside world would indeed have been lifted.

Rothlan's horse shifted beneath him as it eyed the steep slope to the water but he gave it no time to think. Urging his mount down the brae towards the river he splashed across to the far bank. His men crossed after him and let out a ringing cheer as they reached the other side. They were across, the spell that had held them within Jarishan had been broken and they were free.

Rothlan dismounted and, making his way to a grassy knoll, surveyed the sea of faces that surrounded him. "I must now ask you to put your trust in me! I have a spell to cast that will take you to Edinburgh. As I make it, I want you to think yourself inside the hill in Edinburgh called Arthur's Seat. You all know it of old!"

There were nods and murmurs from his soldiers. It was many years since they had been in Edinburgh but no one could forget the great hill shaped like a sleeping dragon that dominated the city.

"Think of its tunnels as you hear the words of the spell and it will transfer you there in seconds! Trust me!"

Rothlan shut his eyes and chanted the words of the spell and in an instant he, and his men, disappeared.

16. Emergency Flight

At around the same time as Lord Rothlan and his army opened their eyes to find themselves inside Arthur's Seat, three pigeons landed neatly in the courtyard of Sir James's distillery where Jamie Todd had been waiting for them patiently.

"Sir James will be pleased to see you," he said kindly as he bent down, arm outstretched, so that they could perch on his sleeve.

Fervently hoping that no one would notice, he carried them carefully up the stairs to Sir James's office and looked round helplessly for somewhere to put them. The pigeons solved the problem for him by fluttering to an upright chair and perching on its back.

Sir James stood up, eyeing them warily and almost jumped out of his skin as Archie materialized from the back of one of the pigeons.

"Archie! I ... er ... how are you? I ... I'm sorry ... it's just that I still can't get used to the way you change around so much."

"That's all right, Sir James. It's easily done and you'll soon get used to it. Hamish and Jaikie here," he indicated the other two pigeons, "have come to take you into the hill." He moved over to one of the pigeons who obligingly stuck a foot out. Tied to its leg, Sir James noticed, was a little bag.

"Is that a message for me?" he asked interestedly.

"No, it isn't a message," said Archie. "It's a jewel. A firestone!"

"Ah, yes! I remember," nodded Sir James. "When Arthur cried, his tears solidified." He looked at it closely as Archie emptied it out of the little bag and into the palm of his hand. "It's ... different, isn't it? It seems to contain moving fire." He touched it with his finger. "How wonderful! Quite unlike any jewel I've ever seen."

Sir James was unsure as to whether or not the fire-stone was intended as a gift and hesitated to ask. He was glad, however, that he'd said nothing when Archie remarked, "It's not only beautiful, Sir James, it's a magic stone, and I brought it because without it you won't be able to merge with this pigeon."

Sir James almost fell over. "Merge with what?" he asked faintly.

"Merge. With this pigeon."

"Me! Merge with ... with that pigeon! What *are* you talking about?"

"Well, you see, the park is full of policemen looking for Arthur. They know something is going on but they're not quite sure what and they're keeping watch. So Hamish and Jaikie have come to take you in with them."

"Quite frankly," said Sir James, looking in horror at the pigeons, "I don't think I want to try this merging business. How on earth am I going to get my bulk into that pigeon?"

Hamish then demerged from his pigeon, looking strained and anxious. "Sir James, please. You must come. We badly need your help, you don't know how much! Many things happened after you and Arthur left last night and the MacArthur needs to see you, especially now that the Ranger can't come."

"What's the matter with the Ranger? He was fine when he dropped me here an hour or two ago."

"The Ranger's had to go back to work, to help organize the police patrols. He's taken Neil and Clara out with him, though, so that they can slip into the hill while no one's looking."

"And you really want me to do this ... merging? Won't it hurt the pigeon?"

"The pigeon will know nothing about it, Sir James. Just impose your will on it and it will fly with us," instructed Hamish.

Sir James looked at Jamie helplessly. "What do I have to do?"

"Put the firestone in your pocket, Sir James," urged Archie. "Put it somewhere safe, so that you can't lose it. The power of the stone will allow you to merge with the pigeon."

Hamish went up to his pigeon, put both hands firmly on its back and disappeared. "Just think yourself into it," advised the pigeon, "and you'll be fine."

Feeling a complete fool, Sir James moved behind the pigeon that Archie had materialized from and put his hands on its back. He felt the warmth of its body and the softness of its feathers and all of a sudden he was seeing the world from his perch on the back of the office chair.

"You did it, Sir James," said Archie approvingly. "Now come out of it. Draw your mind together and step out of its back."

Sir James suddenly appeared before them again and looked around in amazement. "I didn't feel a thing!" he said in astonishment.

"Okay!" said Jaikie, "now that you know how, let's go!"

"Right, Jamie," said Hamish. "Take us outside into the yard and we'll be off."

"Are you sure you're all right, Sir James?" whispered Jamie, negotiating the steps carefully.

"So far I feel fine but I'm not sure what flying will be like!"

"Don't worry," answered Jaikie, "you'll take to it like a duck to water."

Sir James fluttered anxiously on Jamie's arm as they reached the yard. With his heart in his mouth, he watched as the other two pigeons flew up into the air but was not at all surprised that his seemed disinclined to fly. Maybe I'm too heavy for it he thought dismally, gazing up at the other two as they fluttered around him.

Jaikie swooped low. "Make the bird do what *you* want," he said. "Come on, Sir James, *fly!*"

As Jamie and Archie watched anxiously, Sir James concentrated his mind and, miraculously, it worked. His pigeon soared into the air and all of a sudden he was flying. He felt his wings beating strongly; he was part of the bird. Below him the buildings that fringed the park spread before him and, intrigued at the sight of the Palace gardens, he veered towards them.

At that moment both Hamish and Jaikie streaked across his path, giving him such a jolt that he almost forgot to flap his wings.

"Where," screamed Jaikie, "do you think you're going?"

"Follow us!" urged Hamish, flying alongside him. "Keep with us and for heaven's sake, don't stray! Remember that we share the same airspace as hawks and buzzards! You really mustn't go off on your own! Stay alert, Sir James!"

After his first wild sortie, Sir James settled between Jaikie and Hamish. Flying was a marvellous experience, he decided, admiring the green sweep of the slopes of the park, the glimpse of the lochs and the red mass of Salisbury Crags.

He was about to speak to Jaikie and Hamish when he realized to his horror that they had disappeared. Flapping around wildly, he remembered what they had said about hawks. But surely he would have noticed if a hawk had caught them? Suddenly, they appeared out of nowhere on either side of him.

"You were supposed to be watching us, Sir James," chided Hamish gently. "We dived for home and you ..." he paused, "you flew straight on! Ready now, dive!"

While Hamish and Jaikie feathered their wings and swooped gently earthwards, Sir James, on a complete high, pulled his wings back euphorically and went into a dive that would have done credit to a hawk.

"For goodness sake!" muttered Hamish, appalled. "Would you just look at him! If he hits the ground at that speed, he'll make a hole six feet deep!"

Jaikie didn't hear him. Realizing that Sir James's daredevil antics could result in mashed pigeon, he snapped his wings back and dropped like a stone after him.

"Feather your wings or you'll hit the ground," he shrieked, as Sir James, seemingly hell-bent on his own destruction, continued to hurl downwards at increasing speed. Jaikie's words hit home, and as the ground started to loom frighteningly large beneath him, Sir James levelled out frantically and, with only a few feet to spare, made a disgraceful landing that involved a few bounces and a couple of cart wheels.

As he lay panting, wings outspread, on the grass, Hamish and Jaikie landed beside him in a state of complete mental exhaustion! Nerves utterly frazzled, they heaved a sigh of relief as Sir James righted himself and fluffed his ruffled feathers, seemingly unaware of the havoc he had caused. Jaikie and Hamish exchanged a look that spoke volumes.

"That was wonderful!" said Sir James, hopping happily over the grass towards them. "You know, I wouldn't mind doing it again. Do you think that one day ..." he enquired eagerly, "it might be possible to merge with an eagle?"

Jaikie lifted his eyes to the heavens. That was all he needed! "You'd better talk to Archie about that," he said, a tinge of sharpness creeping into his voice. "He's always harping on about being an eagle!"

"Aye, and let's face it, Sir James," adjured Hamish, "you've still got a lot to learn about being a pigeon!"

Jaikie fluttered towards what looked like a rabbit hole. "Now," he said turning to Sir James, "this is the last part of the journey. You just let yourself drop down this hole and when I say 'now' you start flapping your wings like mad, okay?"

It was not a nice experience. Even though Sir James was cushioned from the sides of the shaft by the other two pigeons, the sensation of dropping into a black void was dreadful.

"Now," yelled Jaikie, and Sir James flapped his wings frantically as he remembered his instructions. Much to his relief, it seemed that his journey was really over, as the shaft brought them straight into the middle of the main cavern where the MacArthurs huddled round their chief. Sir James sensed a feeling of deep gloom as he demerged and made his bow to the MacArthur and Lady Ellan.

"Sir James!!" Neil and Clara rushed forward to grasp his hands. "Sir James, you were a pigeon! How did you do it?"

"What was it like?" asked Neil enviously. "Did you really fly in the air?"

"I did," said Sir James, smoothing his hair and looking at his arms and legs as if to make sure that he was still all there. "It was a wonderful experience, although," and here he grinned, "I think I gave Jaikie and Hamish a few bad moments! Believe me, there's more to being a pigeon than meets the eye!"

Lady Ellan, glancing from Jaikie and Hamish to Sir James, raised her eyebrows and hid a smile as she stepped forward to welcome him.

"I'm so glad you were able to come," she said, shaking hands with Sir James. "We are in serious trouble and we badly need your help."

"Jamie mentioned something about treasure and stolen jewels?"

"I suppose they are jewels, but actually firestones are much more than that. They are magic stones and have powers of their own. We kept ours with the rest of Arthur's treasure and, I must admit that over the years we tended to forget that they were there. Those stones given to us by the Lords of the North were imbued with very strong magic. A necklace, a belt and a ring, all studded with firestones, were the most powerful. As my father told you earlier, they kept the shield in place around Lord Rothlan's lands. They also protected us here in the hill. Now the stones have been stolen and although we are still searching the hill, we know that they have gone."

"You might still find them," Clara said seriously, looking round at the vastness that surrounded them. "The inside of the hill is huge!"

Lady Ellan smiled. "We know that they have gone because our own power is waning. We feel their loss within us!"

"Rothlan's at the bottom of all this!" snarled the MacArthur, sunk in gloom. "You mark my words!"

"It's all my fault!" Hamish interrupted, wringing his hands. "When Arthur left the hill, I should have gone to his cave to take the firestones into safe-keeping. Instead, I stayed to watch the police arrive and by the time I reached the cave, the stones had been taken. And I found those!" He showed them a soft, dirty bundle of feathers.

"The bird," gasped Clara, taking one in her fingers and looking at Hamish in alarm, "Amgarad!"

"Yes," sighed the MacArthur. "Amgarad must have stolen the stones and with them in his hands, Jarishan will be open to the world. Rothlan must have been feasting on his anger for years. There will be war and it will be to the hill that he will come first, to take his revenge on me. The irony of it all is that although he doesn't know it, I was the only one who stood up for him when the Lords of the North were deciding his punishment. It was Prince Kalman that did for him in the end. He was determined to see him cowed and controlled."

"What about Dougal MacLeod?" asked Clara suddenly. "He might have gone back and stolen the stones."

"I'm afraid that won't wash, Clara!" interrupted Sir James. "Dougal MacLeod is *not* one of my favourite people but I've known him for years and he is as honest as the day is long; MacLeod's no thief."

A whooshing noise and a frantic fluttering of wings announced the arrival of a pigeon through the shaft. It could barely speak and tumbled over itself in its anxiety to get to the MacArthur. "Rothlan's eagles have come, MacArthur!" it stuttered. "They are gathered in the crags with Amgarad."

At the same time, a commotion at the back of the hall revealed several stumbling, bleeding figures. "Rothlan is here! In the tunnels!" gasped one, making his way to the MacArthur. "We came to warn you! He is here ..."

he gasped, "... with an army. How they entered the hill I don't know, for we have guards posted everywhere. We are trying to hold them back, Master, but I fear they are too many for us! Our power is weak and he is using thunderbolts and strange spells against us."

All eyes turned to the MacArthur who seemed totally dumbfounded at the news. Lady Ellan stood up and paced the floor anxiously. "He is right, Father, our power is nearly gone; we cannot fight Rothlan as we are." She looked round as if hoping to draw help from the air and gestured hopelessly. "Surely there must be some way that we can beat him! There must be!"

"We can't beat Rothlan on our own," growled the MacArthur. "The Lords of the North gave us the stones and they will have to help us get them back, but we must not let ourselves be taken prisoner; Rothlan will bury us in the darkest reaches of the earth if he has his way!"

"You're forgetting, MacArthur," said Hamish, "that we still have the magic carpets!"

17. Magic Carpets

Neil and Clara looked at Hamish, their eyes wide. "Magic carpets!" They looked down in startled surprise at the one they were sitting on. "Do you mean," breathed Neil, rubbing its smooth surface with his hand, "that all these Persian carpets are *magic* carpets?"

Lady Ellan nodded, "Yes, indeed," she said, "but they are not actually Persian carpets, Neil. They are very old Turkish carpets and, after the firestones, our most treasured possessions. If we use them to fly out of the hill, however, we must find somewhere safe to go. And that, I'm afraid, will prove a problem; there are so many of us! Where could we hide until help arrives?"

It was then that Clara had her bright idea. "There's always our school," she said excitedly. "No one's in it. It's the summer holidays just now and the school is empty."

"A school," Lady Ellan frowned. "I don't know. What do you think, Father?"

"I know their school," interrupted Hamish, quickly assessing the pros and cons of the situation. "It's just a short way up the High Street from the Palace. Certainly close enough for us to keep an eye on Lord Rothlan. It would do for a start!"

"It's actually a very good idea," said Sir James, who had also been thinking hard. "The city is full of tourists just now and the Festival will be starting next week. There are very few buildings in Edinburgh that are empty at the moment! The school would be ideal."

"Very well," said Lady Ellan, receiving a grim nod of approval from her father. "Let everyone take a carpet and make ready. Quickly! Sir James, you already have a firestone. Now I will give one to you, Clara, and to you, Neil."

She held their hands. "What you must understand is that they are not just jewels. The firestones are magic stones that will allow you to do many things that humans cannot do."

"Like merging?" said Neil.

"Like merging," she agreed, "but they can be used for other things, too. When you travel on a magic carpet, for instance, the stones will ensure that you and the carpet are invisible to humans when you fly over the city. Can I trust you not to lose them? They are rare and very precious. We only have a few left; those that I am giving you are the tears that Arthur cried yesterday. You must guard them well."

"We won't lose the firestones, honestly!" Clara assured her.

"Here they are, then," said Ellan, putting them in their hands and watching as they both stowed them carefully in their jacket pockets. "Now," she said, "let's find you a carpet!"

Clara thought it the most exciting moment of her life when she walked onto the smooth, intricate pattern of the magic carpet and sat down cross-legged. She grinned across at Neil and waved to Sir James, who was looking more than a bit uncomfortable.

"Don't be afraid," Lady Ellan smiled. "The carpets are always very careful of those they carry. You will never be tipped off, I promise!"

Clara looked round in wonder. Hundreds of carpets were moving from the walls of the cavern, some were lifting themselves from the floor but all were making their way towards their owners. The MacArthurs, Clara noticed, greeted their carpets like old friends and

clambered onto them happily, many piling them high
with odds and ends that they were loath to leave behind.
In a few minutes, the great cavern was awash with
waves of bobbing, floating carpets that hovered expectantly, waiting for the signal to move. Neil watched as
Hamish and Jaikie sailed to the front, followed by the
MacArthur and Lady Ellan. Sir James's carpet then
moved forward and Clara grabbed at hers as she too
started to move through the air. She twisted round to
see what had happened to Neil and, to her relief, saw
that he was behind her. Grinning broadly, he gave her
the thumbs up sign as the leading carpets approached
the entrance to a broad tunnel. The tunnel was not lit
and as her carpet followed the others in, she clenched
her fists and, sitting hunched in fear, stared around to
right and left but everything remained impenetrably
black. The air blowing gently on her cheeks told her
that she was moving upwards for, as the carpet tilted
up at the front, she had to lean forward slightly to
keep her balance. "I'm right behind you, Clara," called
Neil. "You'll be okay, don't worry! The carpets know
the way!"

The carpets certainly did seem to know the way and
as daylight filtered into the tunnel she felt better and her
mood changed to one of excitement mixed with anxiety
as they sailed into the open air. Clara saw the carpets and
people in front of her disappear from view, and gulped as
she realized that she could not see herself or her carpet
although she could still feel its comforting bulk.

Beneath her, she could see the slopes of the Park and
the traffic on the roads. There still seemed to be lots
of policemen on the hill but of Amgarad and his eagles
there was no sign. The flight on the magic carpet was
over far too quickly. Clara could quite happily have
flown on it for days. Idly she wondered what it would

be like if it were to rain and smiled at the thought of sitting on a magic carpet with an umbrella up!

The school, as Hamish had so rightly pointed out, was very close to the hill and already she could see its roofs beside those of the more modern new Scottish Parliament building.

"Now what?" thought Clara, suddenly panic-stricken. "I can't see anyone and I don't know what to do!"

The carpet, however, seemed to have its own ideas and took her along a line of tall windows at one side of the school that were all firmly shut. It then climbed higher and Clara realized that her carpet must be following those in front, searching for a way into the building. She watched as a window opened from the bottom. Who was opening it, she didn't know, but it came as no surprise when her carpet headed for the open space. She ducked her head as it floated gently through and came to rest on the floor of what she recognized as Neil's classroom.

Even as she stood up, Clara realized that she had become visible once more. She turned to see Neil walking towards her. "You okay, Clara?" he asked. "We should have shared a carpet. I didn't know we were going to have to go up a tunnel in the dark."

"I'm fine now, honestly. I just can't believe that this is happening."

Magic carpets were landing all around them and, as their owners stepped off, the carpets flew to the side of the classroom and rolled themselves neatly against the wall. The room, however, was steadily filling up and when she suddenly thought of the janitor, Mr MacGregor, Clara began to think that maybe her bright idea hadn't been quite as bright as she had originally thought. Seen in the vast cavern, the MacArthurs hadn't seemed all that many but they already filled the classroom and more were arriving every minute. The room would soon be filled to overflowing!

"Wouldn't we be better off in the music rooms up in the attics, Neil?" she whispered. "Old MacGregor must still be coming into school every day and he's not daft. There's no way he'd not notice!"

Sir James, who was talking to Lady Ellan, beckoned them over and Clara was just about to blurt out her fears when Sir James put his arm round her. "Really, Clara," he said, "this was a brilliant idea of yours. Lady Ellan and I have just been discussing it and she has thought up a plan to make the MacArthurs a little less noticeable. The teachers probably come in from time to time during the holidays and there is a janitor who looks after the school, isn't there?"

"Old MacGregor!" agreed Neil.

"You see, as there are quite a few of us," Lady Ellan gestured towards the milling MacArthurs, "I thought it might be a good idea if we all became mice. In an old building like this, there will be lots of places for us to hide during the day when there are people in the building."

"Mice!" exclaimed Clara. "I don't like mice!"

"But the mice will be us, Clara," she twinkled, "and you don't mind us, do you?"

"No, of course not," said Clara.

"First of all, I'd like you to show me round the school and then I think you had better go home." Seeing the disappointment on their faces, she laughed. "Be sensible," she said. "We can't put any lights on and it's almost dark now. I don't want your parents to be worried about you."

"But how will we get out?" questioned Clara. "The school gates will be locked!"

"You will use your carpets, of course. They will come to you whenever you need them and store themselves here when you don't."

"That will be marvellous," said Sir James, "thank you, Lady Ellan." He turned to Neil and Clara. "I'd like to come with you, if you don't mind. I want to have a word with your father so I can tell him all that's been happening."

"In that case, Sir James," Lady Ellan said, "let me give you a firestone for the Ranger. He may well need to use a carpet at some time."

"That's a good idea. And now that he is involved with the police patrols, I think we could also enrol him as 'our man on the hill.' He's ideally placed to keep an eye open for Amgarad and Lord Rothlan."

"An excellent idea," she agreed, nodding her head in approval.

"Always a good idea to know what the enemy is up to! Another thing I've been thinking about," and here he looked at Neil, "is supplying you two with mobile phones so that we can all keep in touch. I'll have a word with your father about that as well."

"And we'll keep in touch with you, Sir James, through Hamish and Jaikie as usual. Perhaps Clara, you and Neil could visit us tomorrow? Would the janitor let you in if you said you had forgotten some books?"

Neil laughed. "I've a better excuse than that. I'll take a tin of cat food with me. There's a wee cat that hangs around the playground and she's always hungry. MacGregor knows that Clara and I feed her so he won't be surprised if we turn up."

"And," added Clara, "he and our dad play darts together sometimes so it's not as if he doesn't know us."

"Wonderful! Now don't worry about us. We'll go out in the middle of the night and find some mice to merge with. There seems to be a lot of building work going on round about so I think we ought to find plenty."

18. Mischief the Cat

The next morning saw Neil and Clara making their way up the High Street to the school. "Let's hope the gates aren't locked," muttered Neil, as they reached it. But the gates were open and as they strolled into the playground they were amazed at how different the building seemed during the holidays. They walked round to the side door and, pushing it open, tiptoed into the school to look for the janitor.

Clutching the tin of cat food and a spoon in the manner of a talisman, Neil went to the janny's office and poked his head round the door. "Mr MacGregor!" he called.

"I think he must be upstairs," said Clara. "Listen!"

From the top of the school came the sudden sound of doors banging and a great deal of thumping.

Neil and Clara looked at one another in horror. Was old MacGregor being attacked? Neil's heart sank as he realized that the noise was coming from one of the huge attic rooms at the top of the building. He put the tin of cat food on one of the stairs and peered upwards.

"The MacArthurs!" he hissed at Clara, as he started leaping up the steps, two at a time. "Come on, we've got to help them!"

They burst into the music room at the top of the stairs and stopped short in horror. Old MacGregor must have come up the stairs so quietly that he'd taken the MacArthurs by surprise. They certainly hadn't had time to hide. The music room was full of mice — hundreds of them! Grey mice, brown mice and even black mice scuttled here and there as MacGregor whammed the floor with a brush in his attempts to flatten them.

Clara gulped but Neil ran forward and grabbed at Mr MacGregor's brush.

"Mr MacGregor! Are you all right? We thought you were being attacked!" he shouted at the red-faced janitor.

"Can't you see them?" shouted MacGregor. "Just when I get rid of you lot, what happens? The school gets infested with mice!" He threw the brush to one side. "I'll have to phone the Council," he moaned, starting for the stairs. "Get the rat-catcher in! Pest control! You name it, I need it!"

Neil looked at Clara in horror. The last thing they wanted was officialdom nosing its way round the school.

"Why don't you wait for a few days, Mr MacGregor?" suggested Clara. "They might all disappear ... go somewhere else, you know ..."

The janitor looked at her in disgust. "If it were one mouse or even two or three," he snarled, "that might be an option. But did you see them? Thousands of them!"

"Oh, I wouldn't say thousands," said Neil. "Hundreds, maybe."

"And that's nothing to worry about? I'm phoning the Council this minute!" He stomped down the stairs with Clara fluttering after him, wondering what on earth she could do to stop him. At the bottom of the stairs he almost tripped over the tin of cat food that Neil had left behind when they went upstairs.

"What's this?" he asked, glaring at them suspiciously.

"It's food for the cat in the playground," replied Neil. "You don't mind if we feed her, do you? Mum gave it to us."

"Aye! And since when did your mum run this school? I run this school, I'll have you know, and I'm no' having that ... cat ... in ... here!"

He paused thoughtfully. Neil and Clara had already grasped this possible solution but didn't dare make any remark as they watched old MacGregor's brain ticking over.

"Aye, there now. A cat might be just the thing. She's hungry and, let's face it, there are enough mice upstairs to feed her till the end of the summer holidays!"

"That's a great idea, Mr MacGregor," praised Clara, eyes wide. "Why didn't we think of it?"

"Much better than sending for the Council," agreed Neil. "For if they saw all these mice they might think you hadn't been doing your job properly! One or two, maybe ... but hundreds!"

An arrested expression in MacGregor's eyes told Neil that his shot had gone home.

"I'll go and see if I can find the cat?" offered Clara. "She might be sunning herself on the back wall!"

"Aye! Aye! You do that, Clara! Bring her in and we'll feed her in here so that she kens she belongs." He rubbed a hand over his face. "Mice!" he muttered in disgust.

Clara returned a few minutes later carrying the little black and white cat. She was terribly thin and the touches of white on her coat were smeared and dirty. Her bony face and the shadow of desperation that lurked in her eyes showed only too plainly the crushing deprivations of her short life. She trusted Clara, but once inside the school, she took one look at MacGregor and, given the past history of their relationship, went rigid with fear, leapt from Clara's arms and streaked up the stairs with Clara flying after her.

"Leave them, leave them," MacGregor said to Neil. "Maybe she'll go into one of the classrooms and polish off some of those dratted mice. Here now, use this saucer to put the cat food in."

Neil, with visions of the MacArthurs being slaughtered by the dozen, ran to the foot of the stairs and shouted up, "Clara, have you caught the cat?"

"Yes," she called back. "I'll bring her down in a minute. She seems interested in the mice!"

MacGregor rubbed his hands and sighed with relief. The cat would solve all his problems! The mice had been a nasty shock and not his fault, whatever anyone might say.

Clara came down clutching the cat who seemed to have calmed down considerably.

"My, you've got a real way with cats," said MacGregor, looking more approvingly at the cat who lay, purring loudly, in Clara's arms. She put the cat by the dish of food and watched as it quickly cleaned the plate.

"A saucer of milk!" said MacGregor. "I've got milk here for my tea."

Neil stroked the cat who wound her way round his legs and then went over to MacGregor and wound her way round his legs too. And drank two saucers of milk.

"Well, now! She seems to have settled already! She's quite affectionate!" He sounded surprised.

"Why don't you stroke her?" Clara said. "She's really a nice little cat. You'll have to think of a name for her."

"Yes, what are you going to call her?" Neil watched as the cat sat beside Mr MacGregor's sandwiches and looked soulfully up at him.

"She wants a bit of my sandwich! Would you credit that!" He broke off a piece and fed it to the cat, who purred even louder and rubbed her head against his hand. The cat then received another piece and in no time at all, had finished the sandwich.

A terrible suspicion crossed Neil's mind as he looked at the cat and then at Clara, whose face was disarmingly bland. She picked the cat up and spoke to it firmly. "Now kitty, while your new master is thinking up a name for you, I'm going to give you a *nice* bath!"

Neil watched the cat's reaction to this announcement with interest and promptly had his suspicions confirmed. The cat gave Clara what could only be described as a dirty look and stoically endured the rigours of a bath in one of the wash-hand basins in the girls' toilet. "There you go," said Clara, rubbing it briskly dry, "much better!"

"What a difference!" MacGregor almost smiled at it. "I wouldn't have given you tuppence for that animal a minute or two ago, but now ... well, it looks more like a proper cat! Although there's a real spark of mischief in its eyes, isn't there? Maybe I'll call her Mischief," he said. "How's that for a name?"

Clara looked doubtful and glanced at Neil, who shrugged. Neither of them thought much of it but MacGregor obviously thought he'd had a brainwave.

"Come here, Mischief!" he said.

The cat looked undecided and then rose to her feet, padded over to MacGregor and jumped straight into his arms. It was so unexpected that he almost dropped her, but managing to grasp the tangle of legs and fur he held her like a baby and she purred.

"I think a good name for that cat would be Archie," Neil remarked sourly.

The cat looked at him with a pained expression and Clara tutted disapprovingly. "I think Mischief is a lovely name," she said frowning at him warningly.

"Can we come to see her tomorrow, Mr MacGregor? We'll bring some more cat food."

"Oh, I'll be buying her plenty, don't you worry about that, but you're more than welcome any time. Aren't they, Mischief?"

And, with a sparkling look of devilment in her eyes, Mischief miaowed.

Dougal MacLeod was also in town that morning although he was in the New Town rather than the Old. For Edinburgh divides itself into two parts; the Georgian and the mediaeval. Although he had started the day in a fairly good mood with the feeling that his troubles were over, he was now becoming increasingly frustrated. The Festival was due to start in a few days, he had a rehearsal to attend that evening and the town was literally heaving with tourists. George Street was no exception and a seething mass of cars was grid-locked round the statue of William Pitt that stood in the middle of the intersection with Frederick Street.

Dougal was wearing the ring, belt and necklace that he had taken from the hill. When he wore them he had a sense of being able to do absolutely anything, but knowing that they were magic stones should have made him more circumspect. Be that as it may, the thought that the stones might be able to alter the course of events never entered Dougal's head as he sat in his car, muttering at the hold up and cursing all three statues that decorated George Street.

"Why don't you just go away!" Dougal muttered under his breath. These, I must admit, were not the actual words he used, but the meaning was the same and the result totally unexpected. There was a tremendous flash, a loud bang and Pitt's statue disappeared.

Dougal sat in his car, his mouth hanging open, staring at the empty space where the statue had stood. Some motorists got out of their cars to view the damage, but there was no damage; not even a hole in the road. Having heard the tremendous bang, shoppers spilled into the street to join the growing group of people that milled around the empty space. The statue of Chalmers also seemed to have vanished and looking in his rear-view mirror, Dougal saw that George IV had disappeared as well! The knowledge that he might have been responsible shook him to the core and the sight of people jabbing numbers into their mobile phones made him sweat, especially as he was sure that a lot of them would be dialling 999. His name might be taken as a witness at the scene of the crime! Dougal's brain went into overdrive!

Suddenly he realized that a car had driven out of a parking place and he swerved in to take its place. He relaxed! No one could take his name and address now! Sticking a "pay and display" ticket on the car, he automatically looked at his watch to note the exact time. Half past twelve already. He'd been in town for longer than he'd thought.

Now that no one could associate him with the disappearance of the statues, his mood changed to one of elation!

Glancing down Frederick Street to Princes Street Gardens and the towering ramparts of the castle, reminded Dougal of the needs of his precision marching team and his ongoing battle with Colonel Jamieson, whose sharp retort to what he'd thought a perfectly reasonable request, still rankled. As Dougal gazed at the rounded curve of the Half Moon Battery his habitually sour expression changed to one of undisguised glee. He touched the necklace of stones under his shirt. Could he do it, he wondered?

It has long been the custom in Edinburgh for a gun to be fired from the castle at precisely one o'clock every day. American tourists tend to duck and run for cover as the report echoes through the centre of town but hardened Edinburgh citizens merely flinch and check their watches. Dougal gazed raptly at the castle, muttered under his breath and waited.

The fact that the one o'clock gun had fired from the castle twenty minutes early, caused utter chaos in Princes Street as half the population stopped abruptly to change the time on their watches and then realized that they couldn't be wrong by twenty minutes! Neither did it go down at all well in the castle itself although those on Princes Street were too far away to hear the Colonel's roar of fury.

Needless to say, the disappearance of the statues in George Street made the headlines in the evening paper. Theories abounded and many people associated the firing of the gun with the bang that had heralded the statues' departure. Sir James, however, did not make that mistake. He read the newspaper report as he was getting ready to give the commentary at the Tattoo and flinging the paper down, phoned the Ranger.

It was Neil, however, who answered.

"Neil, if you don't have an *Evening News* in the house, will you go out and buy one? I want to see what your father makes of the lead story," instructed Sir James.

"Is it about the statues disappearing from George Street?" Neil queried. "There was a bit about it on the news."

"Statues as solid as those in George Street don't just vanish into thin air, Neil. Someone made them disappear and my guess is that it must have been Dougal MacLeod!"

"MacLeod?" echoed Neil. "But why would he want to make the statues disappear? It doesn't make sense!"

"The point is, Neil, that he seems to have had the power to do so! I don't think that Rothlan has the fire-stones after all. I think MacLeod took them!"

"Really!" said Neil. "That means that Rothlan doesn't have the power that the MacArthur thinks he has!"

"Look, Neil, I'm on the point of leaving for a Tattoo rehearsal at the Castle so I'm really pushed for time. Could you go to the school and tell the MacArthur? If MacLeod does have the firestones then we stand a good chance of getting them back!"

"I'll go there now and see if I can see the cat," said Neil.

"Cat?" repeated Sir James.

"It's a long story," laughed Neil, "and it involves Archie!"

"I'll hear about it tomorrow! If you come to the distillery we can lay our plans there. Would ten o'clock be all right?"

"Fine, I'll tell the MacArthur. We'll be there and Dad, too, if he can make it. Good luck with your rehearsal."

"Just a minute, Neil. I've been given a few tickets for the Dress Rehearsal tomorrow night. I was wondering if you and Clara might like to come?"

"That'd be great!"

"I'll give you the tickets when I see you tomorrow then. Bye!"

19. Nightmare Times

Dougal MacLeod returned to his flat later that evening, totally euphoric at his success in the Tattoo rehearsal. His fear that Sir James might accost him had proved unfounded and his team had performed well. If it crossed his mind that the jewels were responsible for the almost magical confidence that had pervaded the team's actions, he dismissed it from his mind. They had always been good but tonight they had been perfect. Dougal ran up the stairs to his flat, his eyes alight with pleasure.

Perhaps it was the excitement of the rehearsal, but Dougal found it difficult to sleep that night. He tossed and turned for what seemed like hours before he managed to drift off and, as his mind relaxed, his dreams became nightmares filled with disappearing statues and the dreadful sight of Amgarad swooping towards him in the dragon's cave. In the early morning he awoke with a sudden jerk as the scraping of Amgarad's talons at the window penetrated his consciousness and pitched him from his nightmare to something that was all too horribly real. His heart pounded in alarm as he made out the fluttering black shape of the bird against the dawn light and, terrified, he held the bedclothes tightly under his chin until Amgarad gave up and dropped from sight.

Unable to think of sleep after that, Dougal got up and went to the kitchen where he nursed cup after cup of coffee as worry gnawed at him. He did not know how the bird had found him but he knew only too well what it was after! The jewels!

He laid them on the table before him then holding them up so that the fiery stones ran in a glittering stream through his fingers, spoke softly to them. "Stones, protect my house if you can, and protect me too from my enemies."

Wandering through the dark tunnels of the hill, Lord Rothlan didn't think highly of his new domain. Even Jarishan at its coldest, he reckoned, was better than this dark, gloomy labyrinth! Entering the cavern where the MacArthur had held court, he glanced around indifferently and walked up to the carved chair.

"Make this place habitable and for goodness sake light some torches," he instructed his servants, pointing to sconces in the wall. "Bring what little furniture the dragon left in one piece. Tables, chairs, anything!" He shook his head in disdain as his valet arranged cushions on the chair so that he could sit comfortably.

"First of all, I should like to talk to Amgarad," he instructed the bowing servant. "I must hear his report before I make my plans. Is he here?"

"Master, he is here. I saw him feeding in the kitchens only a few minutes ago."

"Let him finish," instructed Rothlan. "Poor Amgarad. He has endured much since leaving Jarishan."

When Amgarad finally entered the cavern, feeling much better after a good meal, he hesitated to disturb his master who, surrounded by his officers, was deep in discussion. Rothlan, however, caught sight of him and beckoned him forward.

"My brave Amgarad!" he said, rising to his feet and greeting the bird warmly. "Welcome to our counsels. We were discussing the MacArthurs but their whereabouts can wait. Your news is much more important."

Amgarad swelled with pride at his master's words. He knew that he had done well but his pleasure was marred by the knowledge that he had failed to secure the firestones. If only he had managed to get to the dragon's treasure before the thief!

"Let us hear your report, Amgarad."

So much had happened that Amgarad hardly knew where to begin but he gave a succint account of his adventures and was flattered by the respect of the captains who, as yet, knew nothing of the changed world outside; for by this time Amgarad had become positively blasé about the traffic, and the growling red monsters that roamed the streets of the capital now held no fear for him.

"Early this morning," he concluded, "I went to the house of the thief but I could not enter for the windows were locked against me and there was no way in. But I could take you there, Master."

"The world, you said, has changed, Amgarad. Will people not look at me and remark my clothes? They are not as people wear now, surely?"

This question gave Amgarad pause for thought. He had, on his sorties into town, noticed many strangely-dressed people walking the streets of Edinburgh and had not judged them a threat since the ordinary citizens of the town totally ignored them. If people could walk round half-naked with pink hair and safety-pins piercing their noses then his master, in Highland dress, would excite little attention in a city where tumblers, jesters and musicians performed on every street corner. He had, of course, never heard of the Edinburgh Festival and did not know that for three weeks every year, hundreds of performers converge on Edinburgh from across the globe.

"Your clothes will not be remarked, Master. There are many in town whose dress is more outlandish. The thief's house is in Hunter Square by the old Tron Kirk. His stair has a red door."

"You have done well, Amgarad," Rothlan nodded approvingly and, glancing round the cavern distastefully, shook his head. "I will be glad to get out of this underground prison for a while and after so many years it will be interesting to walk the streets of Edinburgh once again."

Several hours were to pass, however, before Rothlan's business was concluded and he was free to visit the town. Remembering the house of the old preacher, Master John Knox, he murmured a powerful spell that landed him on that very doorstep and so busy was the High Street that no one noticed his sudden appearance.

Lord Rothlan was stunned by the High Street! It was not the houses that drew his attention; they had not changed much over the centuries although they were considerably cleaner. No, it was the traffic and the colourful throngs of people that drew his attention. Cars and buses were unknown to him and the fact that even small children were completely unafraid of the massive monsters that growled up and down the street, amazed him. The variety of clothes also came as a considerable shock although this was due in part to the good-humoured competition between two theatre groups who, in full costume, were distributing fliers to passers-by in an attempt to drum up trade.

Reassured, however, that he would not stand out in such a crowd, he started to walk up the hill, glad that the way was familiar. From time to time he looked at the upper reaches of the tenements that line the High Street, remembering the old cry of "Gardyloo" that signalled the filthy Edinburgh habit of throwing dirty water, and worse, from their windows into the street.

The church, now standing at a busy crossroads, was an outstanding landmark and walking round it into Hunter Square, he glanced upwards and saw Amgarad perched like a gargoyle on the roof. Following the bird's gaze, his eyes rested on the bright red door that he had talked of.

"The stair with the red door," thought Lord Rothlan. "Let me see what I can find out!" Avoiding the chairs and tables of a busy café, he walked up to it and, finding that the door opened to his touch, entered the long passageway that led to a flight of stairs. Rothlan paused before a door that bore the name *Dougal MacLeod* and knocked. He knew at once that the stones were within; he could feel their power!

A terrified Dougal heard the knock. He crept to the door and eyed the stranger through the spy-hole. Reading the dark purpose in Rothlan's eyes, he felt afraid. The little MacArthurs hadn't really frightened him at all but he could feel this man's power through the wood of the door. As Rothlan had just invoked a powerful spell that should have landed him inside the door, this was hardly surprising. The fact that nothing happened and he remained firmly outside, confirmed his belief. This Dougal MacLeod had used the stones to set up a protective shield round the house, a shield that even he could not penetrate.

Rothlan left the stair and made his way thoughtfully to the street. His glance and a slight shake of his head told Amgarad that he had been unsuccessful.

20. The Pickpocket

It was mid-afternoon before Dougal had the confidence to leave his flat and that was only because the stones gave him courage. Had the choice been his, he wouldn't have gone out at all, but the uniform he planned to wear that night for the dress rehearsal of the Tattoo had to be collected from a nearby dry-cleaner. Looking from his window, he saw that the streets were busy and eventually decided that, as long as he tagged along with groups of people, he ought to be safe.

Although he suspected that his flat was being watched and peered suspiciously from his window from time to time, he could see no one lurking around outside. Amgarad, perched motionless but vigilant on the pinnacles of the Tron Kirk, was well hidden and the pigeons who flew in at around lunchtime looked innocent enough. Jaikie and Hamish, however, had been at the meeting in the distillery that morning and their errand was serious.

Everyone had managed to attend the meeting, even the Ranger who was tired from working so much overtime. The MacArthur's relief on hearing that it was probably MacLeod who had stolen the firestones had been palpable. He looked at the newspapers that Sir James spread in front of him and agreed that the disappearance of the statues would hardly be Lord Rothlan's work.

"It is much more likely to be MacLeod," Sir James assured him. "Especially the one o'clock gun firing early!" He smiled at the memory. "Jamieson was still spitting with rage about it when I saw him last night although he's no idea how it happened!"

"MacLeod must be wearing the jewels then," Lady Ellan said thoughtfully. "There were three items containing firestones and he took them all: a belt, a ring and a necklace. It is possible that he didn't realize the power of the stones at the time but he must be aware of it now."

"There was a rehearsal at the Castle last night," said Sir James, "and he was there with his team." He crossed to his desk and returned with a glossy Tattoo programme. Turning the pages until he came to MacLeod's photograph, he flattened them out and showed it round. "This is Dougal MacLeod, Lady Ellan. Take a good look at it Neil, and you too, Clara, so that you'll recognize him if you see him. It's very like him, although in the street he won't be wearing his uniform. He and his men gave a marvellous performance last night," he continued, passing the programme round to Jaikie and Hamish. "I'd no chance to speak to him, I'm afraid. Everyone was taken up with the French contingent. A nightmare, believe me! Their horsemen, the Spahis, had to use our moving walkways for the first time last night and we were all a bit paranoid about it. Not, mind you, that I can do anything much if it does all go pear-shaped. The commentator's box is high above the esplanade and I'm actually totally cut off from the performers."

"It sounds exciting," smiled the Ranger. "Clara and Neil are really looking forward to watching the dress rehearsal tonight. It's good of you to have given them the tickets."

"Where does this MacLeod live?" asked the MacArthur, passing back the programme. "We should keep watch on him, Sir James. If Rothlan doesn't have the firestones then he will be searching for them too. He already knows that we don't have them, for had the magic that protects Arthur's Seat been in place then he would never have managed to get into the hill the way he did."

"Would he know that Dougal took the stones, though?" asked the Ranger.

"You're forgetting that Amgarad's feathers were found in the dragon's cave. If there was a struggle between them then Lord Rothlan will know all about Dougal MacLeod," Hamish said seriously.

Sir James picked up the telephone directory and looked through its pages. "Here we are," he said, his finger running down long columns of MacLeods. "MacLeod, Dougal, Hunter Square."

"Where's that?" asked Neil.

"Hunter Square? It's just up the High Street by the Tron Kirk," said Jamie Todd, "at the traffic lights."

Lady Ellan looked up from her study of Dougal's photograph. "My father's right!" she frowned. "I think it is important that this MacLeod be watched." She sat back in her chair, glancing round at them all. "I know that it is difficult and that you're all busy people, but if I use a firestone I can easily make myself taller, you know. Then I'd be able to blend in with the tourists and Neil, Clara and I could keep watch outside his flat."

"And do what?" growled her father, looking at her sharply.

"If I can get close enough to him then I might be able to merge with him and get the firestones back that way."

"Hmmmph! I don't like it, Ellan. Jaikie or Hamish could manage that just as well."

"Dougal would recognize them, though," Neil pointed out. "Don't forget that they caught him in the hill. He would never let them near him."

The MacArthur looked undecided. "I don't want you getting into any trouble. Especially Neil and Clara."

"We'll be fine," Clara said. "There are lots of cafés in the High Street. We can sit outside and keep watch without anyone noticing."

"And Hamish and Jaikie can keep an eye on us, if you like, Father," smiled Ellan mischievously, "as pigeons!"

At the time, Hamish and Jaikie had smiled ruefully, knowing that keeping watch as a pigeon could be a cold, boring business but this time they were far off the mark. Although they had started their journey to the Tron Kirk feeling that it was all a bit unnecessary they quickly changed their minds when they soared over the church and spotted Amgarad. The shock threw them into a panic.

"Did you see him, Hamish?" Jaikie whispered frantically. "Amgarad! Up there on the roof of the kirk."

"Did I not! I nearly fell out of the sky!" came the retort. "Come on! We must tell Lady Ellan!" muttered Hamish. "Didn't they say they were going to sit outside a café?"

Neil, Clara and Lady Ellan were chatting idly over glasses of iced orange juice when Clara gave a sudden yelp and grabbed her ankle. "Ouch!" she cried, rubbing it hard. She peered down. Under her chair, looking up at her apologetically, was a pigeon. "What did you peck me so hard for?" she whispered, glancing at the others to let them know that something was happening.

"Sorry, Clara, but it's an emergency!" hissed the bird.

Under the pretence of feeding him, Neil let Hamish hop onto his sleeve and Lady Ellan bent forward to listen to his words while holding a bit of her sandwich for him to peck. Amid the clucks and the coos, Neil heard the word "Amgarad" and his blood chilled.

"Put Hamish down now, Neil," she said, "we're attracting too much attention! Clara, if you scatter some pieces of your cake on the pavement it will give Jaikie and Hamish an excuse to stay near us. When they flew over the church, they saw Amgarad on the roof. They're pretty shaken!"

Clara and Neil looked at one another in alarm. "Don't look up at the church," Ellan warned, drinking the rest of her orange juice. "We don't want him to know that we've spotted him."

Neil paid the waiter but Clara was so busy watching the pigeons and trying to calm her jangling nerves that Dougal MacLeod was half-way across the street before she noticed him.

"MacLeod!" she said, touching Lady Ellan's sleeve. "Isn't that him? On the other side of the road!"

"Where ...? Yes, I see him!"

Lady Ellan reached out her hand and pressed Clara back into her chair. "Stay still," she muttered. "Someone is already following him!"

Clara scanned the crowd. "The man in the kilt and velvet jacket?" she guessed.

"Yes," Ellan said in a curious voice, "the man dressed as a Highland lord." She stared at the lithe figure that strode behind Dougal MacLeod. "Alasdair Rothlan himself, if I'm not mistaken!"

At her words, Neil and Clara paled and the pigeons, hopping swiftly under the nearest table with more speed than grace, peered out anxiously from behind its legs. Ellan rose calmly from her chair, her face set. "Come, we mustn't lose them." She bent to the pigeons, "Hamish, you go to the school and tell my father what is happening. Jaikie, you keep watch here. We are going to follow Rothlan!"

Dougal MacLeod, meanwhile, walked nervously towards the dry-cleaners and pushed the door open. Its bell jangled noisily as he entered and then rang again

as someone followed him in. He turned and his heart
sank in fear, for the man standing behind him was none
other than the man who had knocked on the door of his
flat that morning. He turned to face old Jeanie at the
counter, his face suddenly grey.

"Mr MacLeod!" Jeanie greeted him cheerfully. "You'll
have come for your uniform! I have it all ready for you."
He didn't reply and as he was usually pretty taciturn,
she chatted on regardless. "Aye! You'll be needing it for
the dress rehearsal up at the castle tonight. I heard all
about how well you did last night from my son. He's
one of the security guards at the Tattoo, ye ken, and
he said that he thought your marching was the best bit
of the whole show." As he made no reply to this comment she peered up at him, for she was a small body,
and said, "Are ye feeling all right, Mr MacLeod? You're
looking a wee bit pale. Now, let me see! That'll be four
pounds fifty."

Dougal dug in his pocket and paid her, hardly noticing what he was doing. He folded the uniform in its
plastic bag, hung it over his arm and left the shop,
conscious that the stranger had followed him out and
was moving very close to him. "He's trying to merge
with me," thought Dougal in horror. "Get away from
me! Get away!"

All of a sudden the man vanished. Dougal looked
round and seeing that he was alone, felt as though an
enormous weight had been lifted from his shoulders.
The stones had once again worked their magic. A great
wave of relief washed over him. With the jewels on him,
he truly had nothing to fear. He walked on, his heart
light and his guard down. So confident was he that he
did not notice Neil and Clara as he walked back down
the High Street, nor Lady Ellan as she, too, took advantage of the crowds of tourists to try to merge with him.

It was impossible. She fell back and murmured to Clara. "I can't do it! I can't merge with him. He is using the firestones as protection. Did you see how he made Lord Rothlan disappear?"

"Yes, and the amazing thing was that no one seemed to notice!"

"The tourists were all watching the street-performers, that's why. Look over there! A fire-eater!"

Dougal, too, had stopped to watch the fire-eater as he thrust burning brands down his throat and, quite by accident, his eyes rested on Clara. With her brown hair and startlingly blue eyes, she was an exceedingly pretty child, and he had no difficulty in placing her as one of the children that had been with Sir James when the dragon had taken to the air.

Now the look of recognition in a person's eyes is involuntary and cannot be hidden. Clara saw it flash across Dougal's face and although she did not know how he knew her, it was obvious that he did. Fear gripped her. What if he made her disappear like Lord Rothlan? Instinctively she moved closer to the woman standing next to her, more in an attempt to hide from Dougal than anything else, and promptly merged into her. Ellan, who had been standing beside her, blinked as she realized what had happened and eyed the woman worriedly. Was Clara all right in there?

Clara had never merged with anyone before and although Sir James had told her how easy it was, she hadn't realized just *how* easy! Finding herself inside someone else's body was startling and she was still quivering with the shock of it when she made a discovery that sent her mind reeling. The smart, well-dressed woman that she had merged into had just stolen a purse. "Oh Lord!" she thought. "Of all the people to choose! I've merged with a thief!"

She was just about to attempt to demerge when it occurred to her that she might be noticed and, at the same time, a daring idea crossed her mind. "If only I could persuade this woman to steal the firestones from Dougal," she thought. "But what if I get caught?" Reason told her that it would be the woman who would get caught. Grimly she concentrated her mind and sure enough, she was able to make the woman move closer to MacLeod, who was holding his uniform in front of him, folded over his arm.

In her mind, Clara urged the woman to steal Dougal's belt, and no sooner had the thought crossed her mind that her hand stretched out and she did. So quickly and so cleverly was it done that Dougal felt nothing. Ellan, however, who had been watching the proceedings closely, now stepped forward and as the golden mesh slipped from around his waist and was still in the woman's hand, she held the woman's gaze and deliberately took it from her.

Neil hadn't noticed a thing and was busy looking for Clara when she tugged at his sleeve.

"Where on earth did you get to?" he asked, a look of relief on his face. "I thought you'd disappeared!"

"I did disappear!" she grinned. "Come back over to the café! Ellan and I have news for you!"

The café was almost deserted as they sat down and ordered ice cream. Its customers had left to wander through the market stalls and watch the street performers who continued to compete amiably among themselves for the attention of the crowds.

"We've got the belt of firestones, Neil!" Clara's face was alight with excitement.

"You've *what?*"

"We have the belt! Ellan is wearing it. It was the most fantastic thing, Neil. I merged with a woman who was a pickpocket and I made her steal the belt. MacLeod probably doesn't even realize that it's gone! She was so quick!"

"Fantastic," Neil grinned, pulling in his chair slightly to let a woman squeeze by. The café was filling up once more and the waiters had swung into action, their trays poised as they slipped adroitly between the small chairs and tables.

Clara looked round anxiously at the sudden press of people. "Maybe we shouldn't hang around here, Neil. We should get back to the MacArthur as soon as we can. We're not really safe here and ..." she tailed off and they swung round in alarm as they saw her eyes widen in horror.

Striding across the street towards them was Lord Rothlan, his face set and angry. Clara felt her heart thump alarmingly.

"Lady Ellan," he said, as she stepped forward to meet him. His voice was pleasant enough but his eyes, stern and watchful, never left her face. Ellan met his gaze coolly.

"Lord Rothlan!" she acknowledged.

He did not mince his words but said abruptly, "You have, I believe, something that should be mine."

Ellan raised her eyebrows. "I have nothing that belongs to you, milord."

His eyes narrowed. "That is not actually what I said," he remarked blandly.

She did not answer and his voice when he spoke was icy. "Tell your father!" he said curtly. "Tell him that the firestones should be mine and that I will do anything to get them! Jarishan has suffered enough! Do you understand!"

She held his gaze and nodded. "I'll tell my father what you've said."

He glanced around the café with a grim smile, nodded and left them. Neil realized that he had been holding his breath and let it out in a long sigh. Clara stared at Ellan whose eyes followed Lord Rothlan until he was swallowed up in the crowds.

Clara took her hand. "Do you think he knew that you were wearing the belt?"

"I'm sure he did!"

"Why didn't he try to take it then? We couldn't have stopped him!"

"No, we couldn't, but he knew that we weren't unprotected!"

"Not unprotected?" Neil looked round blankly. "Who ...?"

Clara picked up Lady Ellan's meaning, however. "These people," she said softly, looking round, "all those tourists who suddenly appeared! They're all MacArthurs, aren't they?"

Ellan grinned. "Yes, I knew my father wouldn't let us down. We were always quite safe. Come on, we can go now!" She linked arms with Neil and Clara and together they walked down the High Street to the school.

21. Mobiles and Merging

The first thing Clara saw was the little black and white cat, standing guard on the school wall, squashed between two of the railings.

"Mischief looks *so* much better already," remarked Neil. "I hope he hasn't caught any mice!"

Lady Ellan laughed. "We've given up being mice, Neil, and have put a memory spell on your janitor instead."

"How does that work?" Clara was startled.

"Oh, he see us and then forgets about us."

As they reached the playground, Mischief, who had been keeping watch for them, arched her back and jumped down as they approached.

"What happened?" asked the little cat, frantically. "Hamish came here screaming that Amgarad and Alasdair Rothlan were in the High Street. I've been out of my mind with worry about you!"

"We're all fine, Archie," soothed Lady Ellan, "and we'll tell you what happened in a minute, but first of all we must contact Sir James! Rothlan spoke to us and believe me, he is dangerous and desperate. I'm afraid he might get the ring and the necklace from Dougal!"

Archie stiffened. "The necklace and the ring? What happened to the belt?"

"I'm wearing it! Clara managed to steal it from Dougal."

The cat smiled happily. "Great! Now we're getting somewhere!"

"It's Sir James I'm worried about. We must find him and tell him what has happened. Where do you think he'll be at this time of the day, Neil?"

Neil took a mobile phone from his jacket and dialled a number. "Sir James gave Clara and me a mobile phone each so that we could keep in touch," he explained. "Hello, Sir James," he said excitedly, "we have some good news for you ..."

"We need to meet with you, Sir," concluded Neil, "Lady Ellan is anxious to see you. Yes, yes, okay."

He turned to the others, replacing the mobile carefully in his jacket pocket. "Sir James is still at the distillery. He says to come at once."

"Good," murmured Lady Ellan. "Look, there are some pigeons over there. Why don't we merge with them and fly across to the distillery. It's not far."

Clara swallowed. "We're going to fly?"

"It's the quickest way, Clara. Do you think you can manage? I'll wait until you both merge. Go on, Neil, it's not difficult!"

"What if the pigeons fly away before we can grab them?"

"They won't fly away! Once you decide to merge with them they will stay still for you. Try it!!"

Lady Ellan spoke the truth. As Neil and Clara approached, the birds stopped pecking and allowed them to put their hands on their backs.

"Whoops!" said Clara, with a gasp as she looked at the world through the eyes of her pigeon. She felt quite frightened as everything seemed suddenly enormous. Gingerly she flapped her wings and looked over at Neil who was gazing with some concern at Mischief, who had assumed the proportions of a giant.

"Are you all right?" Lady Ellan asked, hopping over to them. "Come on, then! Let's fly!" With a clapping of wings, the three pigeons soared into the air and circled the school before heading for the green slopes of the park and the grey roofs of the distillery.

The weather was warm and the feel of the air under her wings made Clara wish that she could fly all day. Her sense of smell was strong and the air was perfumed with the scent of grass and gorse as they passed over the park. Not so nice, Clara thought, were the petrol fumes! The journey was all too short and soon they were flying round the distillery, looking for somewhere quiet to land out of sight of the distillery workers. As it was such a beautiful day, however, the windows of Sir James's office were open and they were able to fly straight in.

Sir James rose from his chair, slightly startled at their sudden arrival, and listened attentively as they told him what had happened in the High Street. Lady Ellan removed the gold belt and spread it over his desk so that they could all admire its delicate workmanship. He switched on his desk lamp and in its light the gold filigree, studded with clusters of firestones, gleamed and glittered.

The MacArthur, Jaikie and Hamish arrived on carpets having been told of the meeting by an excited Archie. They were totally overcome at the sight of the belt and thanked Clara profusely.

"Of all the pieces," the MacArthur explained, "it is the belt that holds the most power and with it we stand a good chance of being able to stand up to his Lordship!"

Lady Ellan broke in and said seriously, "Please, Sir James, I think we should try to form some sort of plan to take the rest of the firestones from Dougal MacLeod! He is in great danger, you know. Lord Rothlan is desperate to have them and will do anything to get them."

"Why hasn't he managed to take them from him already?" Sir James sat back in his chair and surveyed them all a trifle apprehensively.

"MacLeod has used the power of the firestones to defend himself and neither Rothlan nor anyone else can take them from him by merging. Clara managed to steal the belt because the stones did not perceive her as an enemy but now that we have it, our hand is considerably strengthened. We now have the power to take the other pieces of jewellery and I think we should move tonight!"

"Tonight?" Sir James sat up as though struck by a bolt of lightning. "No, no, that's impossible! It's the Dress Rehearsal tonight at the castle. He'll be marching with his men in full view of thousands of people!"

"Tell us about this Tattoo, Sir James." The MacArthur settled in his chair and pulled out a foul-smelling old pipe, which he lit with much palaver. "Tell us what MacLeod does, where he enters from and where he goes afterwards. There might be a chance for us to take them and he wouldn't be expecting an attack."

"An attack? You can't stage an attack in the middle of the Tattoo!" Sir James paled at the very thought.

"Don't listen to my father, Sir James," Lady Ellan said hastily, frowning at her father and waving ineffectually at the clouds of smoke that now belched from his pipe. "If you could just explain to us what actually happens."

Sir James steepled his hands and collected his thoughts. "The performers come onto the esplanade from the castle," he began. "Dougal heads his squad of precision marchers. When they've finished marching they don't leave immediately. They line up along one side of the esplanade while the French make their entrance. The French are putting on a sort of North

African pageant and the desert fort is actually erected while MacLeod's men are performing. It's attacked by Touareg who drag the officers' wives to their oasis. The Spahis, however, rescue the ladies, kill the Touareg and it's while they are making their victory round that MacLeod's men march off."

"Didn't you mention moving walkways at some stage?"

"Yes. There are two walkways, one on either side of the esplanade. The Spahis use them to give the impression of making a long trek across the desert. It's all actually working out quite well. The Spahis are fantastic horsemen!"

"Then it might be possible for us to merge with Dougal's men and take the firestones from him when he leaves the castle?"

"I suppose you could," Sir James considered the possibilities. "There is a certain amount of confusion when they leave, I suppose."

"What about Lord Rothlan?" queried Neil.

"I shouldn't think that Rothlan knows anything about the Tattoo," Sir James said. "If he does, then you'll just have to play it by ear, I'm afraid. If I see anything suspicious from the commentary box then the most I can do is divert the audience's attention elsewhere. By the way," he turned to Neil and Clara, "I believe there's a firework display after the performance tonight so you'd better warn your father that you may be a bit late."

"It's ever so good of you to give us the tickets, Sir James. We're really looking forward to the show," said Clara, suddenly mindful of her manners.

"Not at all! It's my pleasure! I hope you enjoy it," Sir James smiled as they rose to their feet and prepared to leave.

The MacArthur put out his smelly pipe and clapped his hands twice. "Carpets!" he called. The magic carpets that had been resting against the wall silently unfurled themselves and sailed forward majestically to hover just above the ground. The MacArthurs climbed aboard but Lady Ellan left the distillery deep in conversation with Neil and Clara.

Sir James watched them from his window with a sense of unease and wondered what they were up to! He sighed, conscious that the evening's performance was now going to prove utterly fraught. Dress rehearsals were unpredictable affairs at the best of times and adding faeries to an already volatile mix was, as far as he was concerned, nothing short of explosive.

22. The Edinburgh Tattoo

It was a fine night for the dress rehearsal and, as usual, the top of the High Street was crowded with coaches and buses, all off-loading their passengers. The road to the castle, which narrows as it reaches the esplanade, was filled by a moving stream of people of all nationalities and ages. Those who had been to see the Tattoo before carried cushions and thick travelling-rugs as well as umbrellas; for the seating is open to the elements and Edinburgh weather can be fickle.

Sir James watched the stands as they started to fill up and glanced again through his notes. He was generally nervous at the beginning of each performance and knowing that the MacArthurs had a plan of their own made the tension worse. However, his worries disappeared as the dress rehearsal swung into its routine. The crowds responded enthusiastically to the massed bands of the Highland regiments and, as the performance progressed, thoughts of the MacArthurs drifted to the back of his mind. It was only when Dougal's troupe of precision marchers started their routine that he felt a sudden sinking feeling in the pit of his stomach. Watching anxiously from his vantage point high above the esplanade, he kept up his commentary and, as they finished their intricate manoeuvres to rapturous applause, checked that they moved into their pre-arranged position. While the spotlight had been on the marchers, the desert fort had been swiftly erected and all that remained was the positioning of a few fake palm trees in the middle of the esplanade, to provide a desert oasis for the Touareg.

Although nothing untoward seemed to have happened, the opening moves in the drama that was about to take place, had actually already been made. Unnoticed by Sir James, two pigeons had just flown down from the castle and were now perched close to the mechanism that controlled the two walkways. Walkways that had already been started and were moving round slowly.

Neil looked anxiously at the mechanism. He and Clara had inspected it earlier with Lady Ellan and discovered that it was simple in the extreme. Although controlled from the commentary box, there were also manual controls — three buttons labelled *slow, medium* and *fast*. Despite himself, Neil grinned. The Spahis were in for a shock!

The pageant went well! At least at the beginning!

The audience gasped as clever lighting effects transformed the esplanade into a desert of golden sand. The drama began when the Touareg erupted across the castle drawbridge on their camels and charged towards the fort, their striped robes fluttering in the wind. Fascinated, the audience watched as, firing wildly, they deployed round the fort's crenellated walls. It was exciting, picturesque and colourful. The audience loved it!

Everything, actually, went according to plan until the Touareg stormed the fort. It was when they dragged the women out of the great double doors that things started to go fundamentally wrong, for the women were supposed to be taken across the desert to the oasis and tied to the palm trees. The Touareg, therefore, were astonished to find that this particular aspect of their script seemed to have changed overnight! Instead of allowing themselves to be bundled onto the backs of the camels, the women dealt them a few hefty, well-chosen blows, knocked them off their feet and took off across the esplanade in all directions. The audience, not unnaturally, cheered them on! Unable to do anything else under the circumstances, the hapless Touareg scrambled somewhat dizzily to their feet and chased after them.

The spotlights then picked out the Spahis, coming across the drawbridge at a smart canter. Although they looked alarmed at the unexpected developments going on in the middle of the esplanade, they decided to play their part by the book and trotted unsuspectingly onto the moving walkways.

This was what Neil and Clara had been waiting for! Once the horsemen were on and moving at a steady trot, they went into action. Neil flew up, perched on the mechanism and pressed the button that said *fast* with his beak. The result was nothing short of spectacular! As the walkways zoomed to full speed the horses, out of a sense of sheer self-preservation, increased their pace to keep their footing. In the commentary box, Sir James shut his eyes for a second in disbelief. This was all he needed! He stared, utterly appalled, as the entire contingent of Spahis crouched desperately over the necks of horses that were now stretched at full gallop.

"Do something!" he snarled at the engineer who was frantically pressing the remote control buttons. Even as he said it, however, Sir James knew that it wouldn't work. The MacArthurs would have seen to that. Helplessly he waited to see what else would happen. The audience, thinking it all part of the act, cheered the thundering horsemen wildly and certainly, as a diversion, the Spahis proved their worth!

Sir James, meanwhile, was scanning the esplanade whilst keeping up a fairly casual commentary designed to convey the impression that nothing untoward was

happening. What he saw filled him with foreboding
for, in front of his fellow officers, Dougal MacLeod was
being mugged by a couple of Touareg and a woman who
looked suspiciously like Lady Ellan! And his men were
doing nothing about it!

"MacArthurs!" thought Sir James. "They must have
merged with them!"

As Dougal was thrown to the ground and roughly
manhandled, Sir James caught the glint of gold as Lady
Ellan slipped the necklace over her head and the ring on
her finger. He sighed with relief! Now that she had all
the firestones, surely things would return to normal.

Given the situation, this was something of a forlorn
hope, for no sooner had Lady Ellan put on the jewels
than Lord Rothlan materialized in all his finery and
moved towards her. As several of the Touareg rushed
to protect her, he raised his arms into the air and at
his signal, the sky suddenly darkened, despite the glare
of the lights. An eerie silence descended and a wave
of unease swept the audience as, out of the darkness,
loomed the enormous, dreadful shapes of the eagles.
Headed by Amgarad, they swept down, wings drawn
back and talons outstretched, to attack the Touareg
guarding Lady Ellan.

Lord Rothlan, however, had been at a disadvantage
from the start. Unaware of the sequence of events in
the Tattoo, he had been reduced to playing the situation by ear and it was not, perhaps, surprising that
he had severely miscalculated the timing of his move.
Ellan, now wearing the necklace, belt and ring, was all-
powerful. Seeing what was happening, she raised her
arms towards the swooping eagles and, in an instant,
changed them into white doves.

Amgarad couldn't believe it! He almost swallowed
his tonsils in rage as he shrank from the size of a

massive bird of prey to a small ball of pretty, white feathers. Incoherent with rage, he hissed and spat in an agony of fury and frustration at being so cleverly thwarted. The audience, however, reassured by the appearance of doves, forgot their feeling of unease and cheered again, impressed by such fantastic special effects.

Neil, who had almost had a heart attack at Rothlan's sudden appearance, decided that another diversion was most certainly called for and promptly jabbed the *stop* button with his beak. Had he pressed *medium,* or even *slow,* the result might well have been different but stopping the walkways altogether had a dramatic effect that quite successfully diverted the audience's attention back to the galloping horsemen. For the abrupt halt of the walkways sent the entire contingent of Spahis shooting off the end of the belts like bullets out of a gun!

Lord Rothlan, though stunned by the transformation of his mighty eagles, was nevertheless a man of resource. When the spotlights veered towards the horsemen, he found himself in comparative darkness and, as the doves fluttered helplessly round his head, it did not take him long to realize just how neatly he had been outwitted. With his face set in lines of fury, he stepped forward and grasped Ellan by the wrists. Sir James saw his lips move as he uttered what must have been a spell. Instantly there was a sharp crack as both they and the doves disappeared, leaving the remaining Touareg milling around indecisively in the middle of the esplanade.

The spotlights, however, were still concentrated on the Spahis as they rocketed off the walkways. It was their superb horsemanship that saved them and it says much for their skill that not one of the horses lost its footing as it was catapulted forward. Once on firm ground, they miraculously recovered their balance and their riders galloped them, sweating but triumphant, around the esplanade to much cheering and applause.

And surely no applause, thought Sir James sourly, had ever been more merited!

The Spahis then reined in their galloping horses and swerved to attack the Touareg who, by this time, were so confused that they forgot to fight back and were ignominiously routed. This ended the French contribution to the Tattoo and left Sir James doing his best to convince the audience that all had gone to plan and shouldn't they give the French a rousing cheer!

After a few more items, the Tattoo drew to a close and as the last pipe band left the esplanade at the end of the performance, Sir James gave a huge sigh of relief. His part in the proceedings was thankfully over, as the firework display had nothing to do with him. He sat back exhaustedly in his chair trying to control his racing thoughts. All in all, he thought they'd come out of the French fiasco relatively well, with few in the audience realizing that there was anything amiss. A lot can be forgiven in a dress rehearsal and they had been a supportive audience. Such lassitude, however, would most certainly not apply to either the French officials or the organizers of the Tattoo, who would shortly be asking some very pertinent questions. Not that that worried him, as the question that dominated his thoughts was the present whereabouts of Lady Ellan!

"I must get in touch with Neil," he thought, and then remembered that Neil ought to be watching the fireworks with Clara. The display had just started with the first starry outbursts streaking the sky with fire.

"Maybe they'll have left for the school now that Lady Ellan has vanished," he thought as he tapped Neil's number into his mobile, hoping desperately that he would answer.

Neil answered at the first ring. He had just demerged from his pigeon and had been about to call Sir James.

"Neil! Where are you?"

"Sir James!" The relief in Neil's voice was apparent. "I'm glad you called! Did you see what happened to Lady Ellan?"

"I did," answered Sir James, keeping his side of the conversation brief as the commentary box hosted cameramen and technicians that might prick their ears up if the conversation became too interesting.

"I hope you don't mind, but we don't feel like watching the fireworks. Getting Lady Ellan back is much more important! What do you think we should do?"

"I can't talk now, Neil, but I think we ought to meet up with her father."

"At the school?"

"Yes, I'll meet you there. It won't take me long to clear up here. I ... Oh no!"

From his vantage point in the commentary box, Sir James's field of vision extended beyond the immediate environs of the castle. There was a long silence as he stared in disbelief at the sight that met his eyes. Whatever else he had thought might happen, it certainly hadn't been this!

"Sir James! Sir James! What is it?" Neil's voice was shrill. "What's happened?"

"I can't believe it!" Sir James was so shocked that he almost gabbled the words. "It's impossible! You'll see him in a minute, Neil! Look beyond the castle ..."

"See who?"

"Arthur!" whispered Sir James in an agony of apprehension. "Arthur has come back! He's seen the fireworks and he's heading this way!"

23. Kidnapped

Rothlan was still grasping her firmly by the wrists when Lady Ellan opened her eyes. She met his gaze squarely and then looked in wonder at her surroundings; she was no longer in the open air and all traces of the castle and Tattoo had vanished. Around her instead, loomed the vast hall of a castle. It was a pleasant room despite its size. A log fire burned in a huge fireplace, and shields and armour decorated the staircase. It was the dark blue and green weave of the curtains, however, that gave Lady Ellan the clue to her whereabouts. Her eyes flew to Rothlan's face, for she knew his tartan. He had brought her to Jarishan!

Even as her lips formed the word, Lord Rothlan released her. His lips twisted in a sneer. "Welcome to Jarishan!" he said abruptly.

Servants clad in his livery entered the hall and stopped dead as they recognized him. From the outside came the rush of heavy footsteps as his captains entered in search of their master.

Their leader, a hefty, grizzled Scotsman, saluted smartly. "Thank goodness you are safe, Master! We did not know if it was your spell or that of the MacArthurs that took us from the hill so suddenly!"

"The eagles, Hector?" Rothlan demanded. "Amgarad! Have they returned?"

Lady Ellan noticed the anxiety in his voice as he asked the question and the relief that crossed his face as the man nodded.

"They have, milord! They are circling outside."

"Good! Let Amgarad enter and Hector, would you ask your wife to come to the castle with some of the ladies. We have," he paused, turning to Ellan, "a visitor. Lady Ellan, may I present the Captain of my Guard, Hector Mackenzie."

Hector bowed, but not before she had caught the expression of amazement that crossed his face.

"Lady Ellan is our prisoner, Hector. She will reside in the west tower. I would be obliged if you would ask your wife to attend her, and perhaps some of the other ladies would make sure that her quarters are suitable."

"Welcome to Jarishan, Lady Ellan," the captain bowed again. "I knew your father well in days gone by and it is a sad thing for me to see his daughter in such circumstances."

Ellan searched her memory. "I do remember him talking of a Hector Mackenzie and an incident involving," she almost smiled, "... a stag, was it not? From Lochiel's estate?"

A broad grin split Hector's face from ear to ear as he recalled the incident and then disappeared as he straightened his face in an attempt to look suitably sober under the sour gaze of his master.

"Aye! Weel!" he muttered. "Fancy the MacArthur remembering that! Er ... honoured to meet you, your ladyship." He turned to Lord Rothlan. "Fine, Master, I'll be telling my wife to come up to the castle right away and I'll pass the message on to Amgarad. Now, if you'll excuse me! Milord. Lady Ellan!" He bowed to her and his master and left by the great front door.

In the sunlit forecourt of the castle, they could hear him calling Amgarad and in a few seconds the door darkened as the huge bird swept inside and landed on Rothlan's shoulder. However, when he saw Lady Ellan standing in front of him he struggled to keep his balance, his eyes flashed fire and his feathers stood on end. Bristling with rage he hissed at her furiously and his master winced as the razor-sharp talons penetrated his jacket. Ellan stood her ground but the bird was such an awful creature that she whitened perceptibly. Even as she stared at him in horror, Amgarad lowered his gaze and turned to his master, whose arm reached up protectively to shield him.

Rothlan indicated the chairs that stood on either side of the massive fireplace that dominated the hall and waited until she had made herself comfortable before sitting down himself. Amgarad settled on the arm of Rothlan's chair, rigid with disapproval at Lady Ellan's presence.

"Meet Amgarad, Lady Ellan. Captain of my eagles. I still call them 'my eagles' although they do not resemble them any more. The fault of Prince Kalman and your father!"

"Prince Kalman, maybe, but certainly not my father," Ellan said sharply. "He told me himself that he disapproved of what happened to your eagles and he remembers Amgarad well!"

Rothlan looked at her from under lowered brows. "Do you expect me to believe that?"

"I am not accustomed to telling lies!" Ellan responded proudly. "I give you my word. He was overruled by the others when the Council made its decision."

"By Prince Kalman!" Rothlan almost spat out the words. "Has he been made Master of the Council yet? That was what he was angling for before I was exiled."

Lady Ellan shook her head. "No, the old men still have the power," she said guardedly.

"You surprise me! I thought he would have been made Master by this time."

"From what I hear, I think he's more or less side-lined the Council ..."

Rothlan snorted. "Kalman always played his own game and even I underestimated his ruthlessness."

"But you betrayed the Council!"

He looked at her thoughtfully and seemed to come to a decision. "That was what Kalman wanted everyone to believe, Lady Ellan. The truth of the matter is that he saw me as a rival. That's why he put the story round that I hated Charles Edward Stuart. All lies to discredit me. I didn't betray the Jacobites — he planted the evidence against me and believe me, it was damning! I can't blame the Council for not believing my story but I think they might have taken my word before that of a Meriden!"

Ellan heard the ring of truth in his voice and met his brown eyes steadily. "You mean ... you supported Bonnie Prince Charlie?"

"Of course I did. He was a Stuart!"

She shook her head in horror. "Then Prince Kalman is more evil than I thought! To have you exiled! It's absolutely monstrous!"

Rothlan shrugged. "He wanted me out of the way and he succeeded! May I know what else he has been up to?"

"He travels round the country quite a lot and his spies, the crows, are everywhere. He's powerful in his own right and people are afraid of him! When I was staying with my mother's family at Machray, I heard rumours ..."

"Go on!"

"Old Agnes — you must remember her? The carpet mender! She disappeared for months and then turned up looking like a scarecrow, saying that she'd been to Ardray."

"Ardray? Kalman's estate?" He pondered the thought. "Well, maybe he had magic carpets to mend."

"Strange, all the same, that he would keep her there for months on end."

"I can't even begin to guess what Kalman's up to but I know he needs watching, just like his father before him. He'd stop at nothing to get what he wants."

Lady Ellan gave a wry smile. "And you?" she asked. "Haven't you just kidnapped me to get what *you* want?"

Rothlan walked over to her and, taking her hand so that the firestone ring gleamed piercingly between them, looked at her steadily. "You are wearing the firestones," he said. "Their magic has imprisoned me and mine for many a long year but now, as you see, it is summer at Jarishan. I told you in Edinburgh, Lady Ellan. The firestones should be mine. I need them to protect my land and my people."

"Why don't you take them from me? You could. Your magic is powerful!"

He looked at her. "Magic is not always straightforward, milady. You must know that. It would be useless for me to take them from you by force. You must give them to me of your own free will for the power of the stones to benefit Jarishan."

Ellan looked appalled. "I can't give them to you. How can I? Their magic also protects us in the hill. Without them we would lose *our* power." She withdrew her hand from his grasp and returned to her chair.

"If you will not give them to me," Rothlan shrugged and moved towards the fireplace, "then I must keep you here at Jarishan." He rested one hand on the mantelpiece and looked at her broodingly. "One way or another, the stones must remain here!"

"My father will come for me!" she flashed at him angrily.

"He may well come for you; but what will he do? While you are at Jarishan, the stones will protect us. You will not be able to use them against me, nor," he smiled sourly, "turn my poor Amgarad into a dove again!"

At this remark, Amgarad made an indescribable noise, hunched his shoulders angrily and dug his talons deeper into the chair.

"Aren't you afraid that I might try to escape?"

"I must, of course, have your word of honour that you will not leave the island."

There was silence between them. Then Ellan nodded. "Very well, Lord Rothlan. I give you my word of honour that I will not leave the island."

"In that case, Lady Ellan, you are free to go where you please."

24. Dragonfire

The sudden bursts of blazing stars that lit the night sky drew Arthur like a magnet towards the castle. Fire after all, was his element and he proceeded to revel in it. His sinuous body swooped out of the darkness and soared over the battlements as he chased and swallowed stars to his heart's content. Although the bangs had startled him at first, it had not taken him long to realize that they were merely the precursor to another feast of fire. He had never, in his whole life, enjoyed himself so much.

Clara sat watching, open-mouthed. In truth, she could not describe how she felt. Shock, horror and wonder were all there but paramount was a feeling of thankfulness and relief. She had not been at all happy leaving him to the not-so-tender mercies of Nessie and she could only feel glad that he was back among them once more.

"Are you still there, Sir James?" Neil was aghast as he watched Arthur's antics.

"Yes, I'm just wondering if we'll be able to cover all this up!"

"We mightn't have to," whispered Neil, looking at the people around him who were staring in fascination at the sky. "The audience doesn't seem to believe that he's a real dragon at all. They think he's part of the show!"

Arthur had a wonderful time as he wheeled and cavorted round the sky, gobbling up rockets and exploding sparks until even he decided that he'd had enough. All of a sudden, he felt the most enormous burp growing inside him and his whole body wriggled convulsively as he spewed the most glorious display of fireworks into the air. For a moment he couldn't believe that he had actually produced the wonderful starry fire that wreathed him in light.

Tentatively, he tried again and blew another burst of glorious fire that sparkled and whizzed round him like Catherine Wheels gone wild! It was then that Arthur realized that he had, at last, grown up and could breathe fire like all the other dragons he had ever heard of. So exciting was this thought that more than anything he wanted to tell his dear friend, Archie. So, with a flick of his tail he left the brightly-lit castle, disappeared into the darkness and flew like an arrow towards Arthur's Seat and home.

Clara and Neil looked at one another in amazement. Arthur's final bursts of sparks had been so fabulous that they had made him seem like a firework himself.

"Wow!" Clara said loudly. "Wasn't that amazing? That dragon really looked real, didn't it? I wonder how they did it?" Her neighbours nodded in agreement. Everyone, after all, knew that dragons didn't exist and it was, perhaps, this ingrained belief that served to relegate Arthur from reality to the higher realms of pyrotechnic engineering!

Jostled by the crowds making their way down the High Street, Clara suddenly grabbed Neil's arm and dived into the narrow confines of Lady Stair's Close. "Carpet!" she commanded, clapping her hands twice as she had seen the MacArthur do. "Go on, Neil! Clap! You know what Lady Ellan said!"

Neil said, "Carpet!" and clapped his hands twice. Looking up at the high walls of the close, he moved further towards the open courtyard that lay beyond. "Do you think they'll come?" he asked doubtfully.

"Lady Ellan said that they would come when we called them, didn't she?"

"Yes, but nothing's happened yet!"

"Give them time! They've got to get here remember!"

The carpets arrived in barely a minute. Neil saw them first and grabbed Clara by the arm as two carpets suddenly appeared and hovered in front of them. Clara recognized the pattern on hers and scrambled onto it. Neil watched anxiously as she promptly disappeared. "Are you there, Clara?" he whispered.

"Of course I am!" she said, her voice coming from nowhere. "Hurry up! Someone might come into the close."

"Where shall we ask them to take us? To the school or to the MacArthur?"

"The MacArthur, I think. It would be useless going to the school if he isn't there!"

Neil clambered onto his carpet and felt it give under him as he sat down. "Take us to the MacArthur!" he instructed. The carpets floated up into the air and soared over the houses, lights, traffic and people of the High Street until the old familiar school building loomed in front of them. This time, the carpets knew exactly where they were going and floated round until they came to an open window. Clara ducked her head as they skimmed through and jumped off as her carpet hovered just feet from the floor. Neil appeared seconds later as he, too, got off. The carpets floated over to the wall, rolled themselves up and settled themselves neatly. Even as they watched in fascination, another larger carpet unrolled itself, hovered for a moment, then sailed out of the window.

"I wonder who it's gone to fetch?" mused Clara.

"Probably Sir James," came the answer. "He wouldn't be able to get into the school otherwise. It's all locked up!"

"Let's call Dad," Clara said. "I'm sure he'll want to be at this meeting."

"Okay," nodded Neil as he dialled the house number. His father answered and, when he heard what had happened at the castle, was more than anxious to come, although he was unsure about using a magic carpet.

"It's easy, Dad! Put the firestone you got from Lady Ellan into your pocket, say 'carpet,' clap your hands twice and it'll come for you. You'd better stand in the garden, though, as it won't be able to get into the house if the windows are all closed."

Clara opened the classroom door and peered into the corridor. Mischief immediately ran up the stairs towards them and purred round their legs. "Hurry up, Neil. Tell Dad we'll see him soon. I think the MacArthurs must be in the Music Room."

With Mischief running in front of them, they climbed the stairs and knocked at the door of the Music Room. It was very quiet and Neil looked indecisive, not quite knowing what to do. Archie, however, demerged from Mischief and pushed the door open. The MacArthurs were all there, sitting round the room in hushed, gloomy silence.

Mischief followed them in. She seemed quite used to the MacArthurs and pleased to see Clara and Neil. They walked towards the MacArthur who was sitting on a chair totally broken with grief.

"We're both very sorry about Lady Ellan, MacArthur," said Neil. "We'll do everything we can to help you get her back!"

"Aye. My dear girl ... in the hands of Alasdair Rothlan!" He shook his head sorrowfully.

Clara looked at him with a dangerous sparkle in her eyes. "Lady Ellan can look after herself," she stated roundly, "and if you ask me, she'll boss that Lord Rothlan around until he'll be glad to let her go!"

"Good for you, Clara! I'm sure you're right!" said Sir James as he entered the room. "A lady of spirit, Lady Ellan!"

The MacArthur, cheered at this attitude, was moved to agree. "Aye! You're maybe right at that! Always an argumentative lassie, my daughter!"

Sir James looked at Neil and Clara quizzically. "I suppose it was the three of you who cooked up the chaos on the esplanade?"

Clara nodded. "We flew into the castle before the Tattoo started. Neil and I were pigeons and the MacArthurs merged with MacLeod's men and some of the Touareg."

"I gathered as much. Poor Dougal! He must have wondered why his men didn't come to his rescue! What I really want to know is how these infernal walkways went so completely berserk! There was no one near them as far as I could see."

Clara and Neil looked at the ground and didn't answer.

Sir James looked appalled. "It was never the pair of you!" he exclaimed.

Neil took a deep breath. "We were pigeons, Sir James. All I had to do was perch on the machinery and jab the buttons with my beak."

"Well, I ..." Sir James shook his head and burst out laughing, just as the Ranger walked into the room. "Ranger, come and hear what your children have been up to."

"What's that?" asked the Ranger.

"I'll let them tell you themselves!" he said with a grin.

While they regaled their father with their exploits and the disappearance of Lady Ellan and Lord Rothlan, Sir James and the MacArthur sat deep in discussion.

"Rothlan must have managed to break out of Jarishan when the firestones left the hill," the MacArthur decided. He shook his head worriedly. "I don't like it! There's going to be trouble! Prince Kalman must be furious! He hates Rothlan like poison, you know. And that's another thing! I haven't heard from Kalman at all! Why hasn't he come to Edinburgh? He should be here, helping us to fight Rothlan. He must know what's going on! Most of the Lords of the North are dithering old fools but not the prince! He's as sharp as they come. If only Rothlan hadn't captured Ellan!"

"There must be secret ways into the hill, surely," Sir James said, looking at him expectantly. "The first thing we have to do is make a plan to rescue her."

"At that moment, the Ranger walked over. "Won't Arthur be able to help?" he suggested. "He's back in the hill now, isn't he?"

"Arthur?" the MacArthur looked blank.

"My goodness! I forgot to tell you!" Sir James clapped a hand to his forehead at his forgetfulness. "Arthur is back! We saw him at the castle. The fireworks attracted him and he had a display of his own!"

The MacArthur sat up, electrified by the news. "Ranger MacLean," he said, "are you seriously telling me that Arthur has come back? He's back and he's in the hill?"

"Yes," the Ranger nodded. "Swooped right over me, he did and disappeared down a tunnel."

Archie leapt to his feet at the news that Arthur had returned to the hill. He jumped up, punching the air, yelling, "Arthur! Arthur's back!" and ran to the door, shouting for his carpet.

The MacArthur ignored him. "But if you saw Arthur going into the hill, it must mean that Rothlan has gone! He and his men must have pulled out of the hill completely." He suddenly rose to his feet and walked up and down, twisting his hands together worriedly. He looked at Sir James, "Ellan," he whispered miserably. "He must have taken Ellan to Jarishan!"

"Jarishan!" whispered Clara. "I've heard of it before. Where is it?"

It was Hamish who answered her. "Jarishan is Rothlan's estate. It's on the west coast of Scotland ... and by the look of things," he surveyed the MacArthur through narrowed eyes, "... by the look of things, I somehow think that we will be visiting it quite soon!"

The MacArthur was so upset that he could barely talk. "Fetch the carpets," he commanded. "We must return to the hill!"

There had been great excitement among the MacArthurs at the news of Arthur's return, followed quickly by a surge of happiness as it dawned on them that they would be returning home. Now their elation had gone completely and they looked at one another apprehensively as they gathered together their few belongings in silence.

Clara bent down and quietly picked up Mischief. Gently, she carried her downstairs to the janitor's office where she had her bed; a cardboard box with a soft cushion and a blanket in it. She hid a smile as she stroked the little cat's head and laid her in the middle of the cushion.

"You'll be all right, Mischief," she assured the little cat, albeit with more confidence than she felt. "Just don't freak when old MacGregor appears in the morning!" And she ran back upstairs to join the others and get her carpet.

Arthur had indeed returned to the hill but his welcome had not been as he had imagined. For the hill was empty, totally empty!

Crying in anguish, he crawled along tunnels and passageways but nowhere could he find any trace of the MacArthurs. He couldn't understand it and became increasingly frightened. His own cave, too, was not as he had left it. His precious treasure was scattered everywhere and, worst of all, the firestones had gone. The thought of living alone in the hill was chilling and he called for Archie until he could call no more.

Shivering and fearful, poor Arthur went round his cave gathering bits of treasure in his mouth until he had heaped it once more into a comfortable pile. Sobbing his heart out and shedding great quantities of firestones everywhere, he lay on his gold, a chastened heap of misery.

It was much later that a slight noise caused him to raise his great head and look towards the entrance to the tunnel. Surely he could not be mistaken! Was that torchlight flickering in the darkness?

Hope sprang in his heart as he lurched off his pile of treasure. A voice, a dear voice that he knew only too well, called out to him. It was Archie! The cave was suddenly filled with the MacArthurs and their torches and Archie, who ran up and flung his arms round his neck. "Arthur! Arthur! You have come back! Please, don't leave us again!"

Standing at the back of the crowd, Neil, Clara, Sir James and the Ranger watched as each MacArthur in turn greeted the great dragon and welcomed him home. Arthur was so happy at this sudden change in his fortunes that he cried even more and drenched everyone in firestones.

Later that night, when everyone else was fast asleep, Arthur poured out the sad tale of his sojourn in Loch Ness to Archie, who nestled comfortably in the crook of one of his spindly arms.

"It is a deep, dark loch, that Loch Ness, Archie. So deep and cold that I thought I would never reach the bottom. And then we had to swim through a tunnel and, ocht ... when we reached her caves, they were dank, cheerless places. Not warm and comfortable like here. And I had no treasure to lie on, Archie, and I did not have you and the others to talk to."

"But surely Nessie had faeries to look after her, Arthur? She could not live on her own!"

"She had faeries, all right! Water goblins!" Arthur shivered at the thought of them. "Horrid, spiteful things! They didn't want me there from the start. They just wanted Nessie all to themselves! And do you know, Archie, over the years they have made her just like them! When I knew her, she was young and full of fun!"

"So you decided to come back?" Archie stretched and smiled happily.

"I missed you, Archie. I missed the others too, of course, but mostly you. I missed our talks and the tales you used to tell me. These goblins did nothing but gossip about one another and Nessie was much the same."

"Didn't she talk about food?" asked Archie, whose mind was never far from the subject of meals. "About what you would have for supper?"

"Fish! We had fish mostly," came the depressing answer. "She ate a lot of fish. In fact, she has such an appetite that it's a wonder there are any fish left in Loch Ness."

"Arthur," said Archie diffidently. "When you left us on the bank of the loch, did you not hear me shout goodbye to you?"

"I did, Archie, but she told me to take no notice. We were together and that was all that mattered. I should

have known then that it wouldn't work, shouldn't I?
She had changed so much!"

His voice tailed off sadly. "Don't worry, Arthur,"
Archie said consolingly. "It's the fault of the water goblins, you know. They enjoy making people as nasty and
mean-spirited as they are themselves. Thank goodness
you left and came back to us."

"I'm sorry about so many things, Archie. About
not saying goodbye to you and taking all Sir James's
whisky and blowing fire and ... *Archie!*"

Archie jumped in fright! "What! What is it? What's
wrong?"

"I forgot to tell you! I can breathe fire on my own.
Just watch!" He turned his head to one side and
breathed a long stream of flames and sparks. "I've
grown up, Archie! I'm a proper dragon now!"

He then regaled Archie with the story of the firework
display at the castle and it was very late when they
finally curled up and fell fast asleep.

Neil, Clara, Sir James and the Ranger also slept in the
hill that night. Jaikie took them through tunnels to a part
of the hill that had escaped Arthur's ravages. It was as
though an old castle had been built within the hill, with
paved floors and dusty, panelled walls. All the bedrooms
were full of ancient furniture; carpets layered the floors
and the walls were hung with old, threadbare tapestries
depicting unicorns and ancient beasts. Each room had a
curtained, four-poster bed made up with fine linen sheets
and piled high with thick, fur blankets. At the sight
of them, they realized just how tired they were. It had
been an exhausting and eventful day and long before the
torches flickered and went out, they were fast asleep.

25. Preparations for War

Next morning, in the depths of Arthur's Seat, Sir James, the Ranger, Clara and Neil sat round an enormous table having breakfast with the MacArthur. The men were deep in discussion and, to Neil and Clara's excitement, they had decided to use the magic carpets to fly to Jarishan.

"There's no other way to move so many troops," declared the MacArthur. "We must fly there by carpet."

"What do you intend to do when you get there?" asked Sir James. "Do you have a plan?"

"I don't know about a plan," said the MacArthur, "but we have plenty of firestones! Dragons, you know, hardly ever cry but Arthur cried so much last night that the whole hill is full of them. We're picking them up everywhere! I have enough to protect the hill while we are away and more than enough to counteract Rothlan's worst spells."

"MacArthur!" Jaikie burst into the room, flushed with excitement. "MacArthur! Thon man that we caught in Arthur's cave ... he's here! He's in the hill and asking to speak to you. And he kens you're here too, Sir James, because he mentioned your name as well."

They all looked at one another in consternation.

"Dougal MacLeod!" groaned Sir James. "It can only be him!"

The MacArthur looked at them appraisingly. "Well," he asked, "will I ask Jaikie to bring him in?"

Sir James threw up his hands in resignation. "You may as well," he said helplessly. "Dougal's up to his eyes in this as much as we are! Let's hear what he has to say!"

MacLeod followed Jaikie into the room a few minutes later, and apart from a plaster over one eyebrow, looked none the worse for his adventure of the previous evening. They all rose to greet him as he bowed to the MacArthur and nodded to Sir James and the others. Although he looked surprised at seeing the Ranger and Neil, he recognized Clara and smiled at her thinly.

"Jaikie!" commanded the MacArthur, "have another place set for breakfast. Perhaps Mr MacLeod would like to join us?"

Dougal held up a hand. "First of all," he said stiffly, "I would like to apologize for taking the dragon's jewels. I don't know why I did it. Something just came over me and I had to have them. I'm sorry I took them and caused you trouble."

"Sit down, man. Sit down!" growled the MacArthur. "We accept your apology and if it is any consolation to you, you may as well know that the firestones themselves are responsible for what you did."

"Firestones? Is that what you call them? You mean they ... the firestones ... wanted me to take them?"

"Aye! They have their own magic, firestones!"

"That ..." said Dougal, looking as though he were about to burst into tears, "is such a relief! I felt dreadful at taking them but I couldn't help myself. I wanted them so much! I'd very much like to make up for what I did. I want to help you in any way I can; if you'll have me, that is."

"You are more than welcome, Mr MacLeod," smiled the MacArthur. "At the moment we look like needing all the help we can get. Now sit yourself down and have a bite to eat."

Another chair was brought and, as Dougal was introduced to Clara, Neil and the Ranger, Sir James made room for him.

"Well, MacLeod," he said with a wry smile as Dougal settled himself and looked self-consciously round the table, "welcome to our little band! I'm not sure what you'd call us but believe me, a more motley crew of respectable scoundrels never walked the streets of Edinburgh! Am I not right?" He looked round for approval and there was laughter and a nodding of heads.

Clara had been watching Dougal carefully and sighed with relief as he joined in. He looked at them all curiously. "There are so many questions I want to ask you all," he ventured, a trifle ruefully, "but I hardly know where to begin!"

Sir James smiled. "It's a long story," he said, "but ask away and we'll do our best to answer!"

"Well, first of all, who was the man on the esplanade? The one who disappeared with the girl? And those awful birds? One of them found out where I lived and tried to steal the firestones."

It was the MacArthur who answered. "His name," he said, "is Lord Alasdair Rothlan and Amgarad, the bird, is his creature. The young lady is my daughter, Ellan. We are just planning a trip to his castle to get her back!"

Clara couldn't help herself. "We're going to fly there on magic carpets!" she announced with a sunny smile that revealed her total satisfaction with this state of affairs.

Dougal's eyes widened and he looked around doubtfully.

Sir James read the disbelief in his eyes and, hiding a smile, remarked casually that they were a very efficient means of travel.

"What I want to know," broke in Neil, "is what happens if it rains? Does the magic keep the rain off or do we get wet?"

Everyone looked at the MacArthur for the answer to this question. "You get wet, I'm afraid," was his smiling reply.

As Dougal helped himself to breakfast, Sir James told him the whole story from the beginning. Dougal was totally flabbergasted! Indeed, had he not been sitting having breakfast with faeries in the middle of Arthur's Seat, he would never have believed the half of it. He shook his head wonderingly throughout Sir James's tale.

"And if you think that's fantastic just wait until you hear about Arthur's adventures in Loch Ness!" Neil grinned.

Soon, everyone was chatting busily as Dougal relaxed and, to his own surprise as much as everyone else's, proved an entertaining talker. In fact he kept the conversation going with such ability that Sir James realized that he had grossly misjudged the man.

Jaikie, however, who was standing by the door to make sure that everyone had what they needed, was aware of what was happening and met the MacArthur's eyes with a smile of understanding. For the MacArthur, looking at stiff, unhappy Dougal, had realized that not only was he lonely but was also intelligent enough to know that he made boring company. So, unbeknownst to all of them, a little magic had flickered across the table, transforming Dougal's awkward shyness to sparkling wit. His success over breakfast left him more than somewhat bemused but by the time they rose to leave the table there was an unspoken understanding among them all that MacLeod was one of them.

Preparations for the journey had already begun and, after breakfast, the hill became a hive of activity. Neil and Clara were bursting with excitement at the thought of travelling such a long way on their carpets and were full of questions. How long would it take? Would they be invisible? Would they fly at night? The MacArthur seemed to have disappeared so they couldn't ask him and as Hamish and Jaikie were busy with the men, they eventually decided to go to Arthur's cave in search of Archie. As they entered the cavern, they saw Arthur rolling happily on his pile of treasure while Archie was wandering around, gathering firestones in a huge sack.

"Can we help you, Archie?" asked Clara. "Everyone is too busy to talk to us today and we've got loads of questions!"

"I was hoping that you'd be able to tell *me* what was happening! I haven't been able to leave the cave. Arthur gets upset if I'm not around!"

"You'll never guess!" said Clara. "The Excise man, Dougal MacLeod, came back into the hill to say he was sorry for taking the firestones!"

"Ach!" Archie muttered, "it was mair like the stones took him! The MacArthur would understand that! Powerful things firestones; they probably had their reasons."

"And," said Neil, "we're travelling to Jarishan on the magic carpets." "Hmm," Archie murmured. "Better take some warm rugs with you then. It can be cold up there and you'll be travelling at night."

"At night?" Clara's voice rang with disappointment. "I wanted to see the scenery. Why can't we travel during the day? After all, we *are* invisible when we fly."

"Arthur isn't, though."

"Arthur!" Clara turned to the dragon. "Are you coming too? Oh! I feel so much better! You'll knock these horrid eagle birds out of the skies!"

Arthur rolled again in his treasure and clawed his way over the piles of gold towards them. Clara wasn't at all afraid of him. Having seen Nessie's sly, predatory look, she knew that for all his size, Arthur was a softie and would never hurt her. Putting a hand on his wing, as she had seen Archie do, she curled up against him and talked to him. Neil lay flat on the pile of treasure beside the dragon, idly letting gold coins trickle through his fingers as he listened.

"Was it very bad for you in Loch Ness?" Clara asked.

Arthur lowered his great head. "It was not nice at all. Cold and dark and wet! And no treasure to lie on and no friends to talk to. And the goblins had changed my Nessie ..." his voice tailed óff sadly.

"Water goblins," remarked Archie in explanation. "Nasty things!"

"What on earth are water goblins like?" asked Neil.

"Mostly wet," grinned Archie.

"And cold," added Arthur, "and they smell; a horrid, musty smell. But to look at, they are small, grey and shiny black. Black, like their hearts. They are not like my MacArthurs at all."

"Didn't they talk to you and keep you company like Archie does?" asked Neil curiously,

"They did not! They hugged their secrets to themselves. It is one of their pleasures to have secrets! They wouldn't tell me anything. They spent most of their time at the bottom of the loch, sifting through the silt. I heard a whisper that Prince Kalman had asked them to search the loch for buried treasure but I didn't believe it. Most likely they were looking for tasty worms. They wouldn't tell me."

"Prince Kalman?" Archie looked at him curiously. "Are you sure?"

Arthur nodded. "That's what Nessie told me. Grechan, the Chief of the water goblins, visited her a while back and she said that he's been using his water goblins to search lots of the lochs round about."

"The MacArthur will be interested to hear that," frowned Archie. "He's been wondering why Kalman hasn't been in touch now that the shield around Jarishan has been broken. I wonder what he's up to. And using the water goblins to help him!"

"Horrible things!" shivered Arthur.

"Well, now that you're back, Arthur, you need never think of them again," Clara said, smiling happily. "You were really fab when you flew over the castle. Just like one of the fireworks!"

"Did you see me?" Arthur was pleased. "I swallowed so many fireworks that I can breathe fire on my own now! I'm a proper dragon at last!"

"Save your fire for Jarishan, Arthur!" advised Archie. "Remember, we have to get Lady Ellan back! No! No! Don't cry again, for goodness sake!" Archie ran forward and hugged Arthur. "It's just that I've picked up so many firestones this morning that my back is killing me!"

Jaikie came into the cavern and, picking up the odd firestone as he came towards them, deposited them in Archie's bag.

"Hello there, Arthur! Welcome back!" He put his arms around the dragon's neck and hugged him. "The hill wasn't the same without you!"

He glanced at Neil and Clara, grinning. "I thought I might find the pair of you here," he remarked. "The MacArthur has decided to wait until after midnight

before we set off for Jarishan so your dad wants you
to go home with him. He's waiting for you in the main
cavern so you'd better get a move on. Sir James has
already left."

26. Journey to Jarishan

By the time the MacLeans and Sir James returned to the hill, the MacArthur's preparations were complete and his men were ready for battle. The huge cavern was filled with ranks of armed troops whose burnished helmets and gleaming breastplates glowed in the torchlight. Silver spears glittered above their heads and here and there a gleam of scarlet flashed brightly.

"Look at their shields," whispered Neil, "a scarlet dragon on a black and gold background."

"It's on all the flags and pennants as well! No wonder Arthur is coming with us!" said Clara. "He's their emblem."

"Their armour is amazing!" whispered Neil. "It looks hundreds of years old!"

"They look wonderful," whispered Clara, suddenly tearful at the seriousness of it all. "Neil, I ..." she gulped, "I hope we win!"

"Of course we'll win," Neil stated confidently. "They look tough and there are hundreds of them!"

Clara touched his arm. "Look, over there. I can see Dad and the others. I think they're looking for us."

They made their way cautiously round the edge of the troops to where their father stood with Sir James and MacLeod. There was a serious edge now to the conversation and even the MacArthur was more abrupt than usual.

"You two will stay out of mischief!" he ordered as they approached.

"We will," answered Neil gravely.

"You understand that your carpets know what to do and where to go? You don't have to do anything; they will take care of you." A smile softened his face, however, as he looked at Clara. "Take care, young lady!"

At a given signal, the carpets were called and poured into the hall in a quivering, excited stream, each one seeking its master.

Clara was trembling with excitement as her carpet zoomed down and screeched to a halt in front of her. She looked at it doubtfully. None of the other carpets behaved like this. Neil's arrived quite sedately by comparison. "Perhaps it's a young carpet," she thought, as she took a fur from a nearby pile and spread it over the carpet.

She was about to climb on, when Jaikie ran up. "Sorry," he muttered. "You should put the first rug on the carpet with the fur-side down. Believe me, the carpet will really appreciate it. They get cold in the clouds and a carpet with a bout of the shivers can be a bit unnerving! And you'll need a couple to wrap round you as well!"

"Thanks, Jaikie," she said gratefully, pulling two more from the pile. As she spread her rug fur-side down, she felt a wave of pleasure ripple through the carpet and smiled as she climbed on. The magic carpets were more alive than she had thought!

"Are you all right, Clara?" called her father.

"Fine," she answered. Neil and Dougal MacLeod moved alongside with Sir James and her father in front. It seemed as though their carpets had been told to stick together for, as the MacArthur set off on the first carpet, all the other carpets followed in order. They flew upwards in single file and, as she ducked her head at the entrance to the tunnel, she remembered how afraid she had been the first time. "How strange," she thought, "I must have got used to it for I'm not afraid of the dark at all now!" The journey to the surface was brief and she was only to catch a glimpse of Sir James before he disappeared and it was her turn.

Neil and her father called out to her from time to time to let her know that they were there, as did Dougal MacLeod, who had not at first believed in magic carpets. Soon they felt comfortable in the knowledge that they were travelling together and Clara amused herself by peering over the edge of the carpet at the hills and rivers that lay in the dark landscape below. Slowly, however, she tired and gradually stretched out in her warm nest of fur to sleep until dawn.

Light was just streaking the eastern horizon when Clara woke with a start as a sudden jolt sent her rolling to the edge of the carpet. "I can't fall off!" was the one thought in her mind as she felt herself tilt over the edge. "Lady Ellan said that I couldn't fall off!" The reality, however, was that she was falling. She screamed in horror. It was impossible to get a grip on the smooth surface of the carpet but, as she slipped into the void, she managed to hook her fingers into its looped fringe. By performing a positive miracle of acrobatics in midair, her carpet slipped itself beneath her once more. Keeping her fingers firmly entwined in the fringe, she relaxed on its smooth length and lay panting with shock and exhaustion for a few minutes before inching fearfully to a sitting position. She was still shivering with fear when she heard Neil's voice.

"Clara! Clara! Are you okay?"

"Yes, but I nearly fell off my carpet," she called back.

"You sound as if you are going further away from me. Tell your carpet to stay close!"

"My carpet's a bit of a rebel," she called back and felt a ripple of laughter run through the carpet as it heard her words. "It knows what I'm saying," she thought. "I didn't really understand that before."

A few minutes later she felt her carpet tilt downwards and realized that they were going to land. Sure enough, as she drew closer to the ground, she saw many of the MacArthurs standing beside their carpets, obviously waiting for the others to land. Clara's carpet brought her to rest beside Sir James and Dougal MacLeod.

"Thank goodness you're all right, my dear," Sir James said. "I haven't seen Neil or your father yet but I'm sure they're fine."

"Neil is, anyway," replied Clara. "He called out to me after we were knocked off. Whatever happened?"

"The MacArthur said that the protective shield around Jarishan is back in place. Apparently we ran into it! He's getting ready to use the firestones to break it by magic."

"Here's Dad now!" said Clara, running forward to hug him.

"Thank heavens you're okay, Clara," he said, holding her tightly. "Have you seen Neil?"

"No, but I know he's fine. He spoke to me but I couldn't see him."

At that moment the MacArthur stomped up.

"Well, that's that done!" he announced. "The shield has lifted already. We'll be able to get moving again once we sort ourselves out!"

"But where are Archie and Arthur?" Clara asked, looking around for them.

"Oh, they'll be well on their way to Jarishan by this time," the MacArthur smiled. "Protective shields are useless against dragons, their magic is so powerful."

27. The Storm Carriers

Arthur had actually reached Jarishan already and as he soared into view over the surrounding hills, Lady Ellan caught her breath and tears shone in her eyes. Arthur had returned! How or why, she didn't know but her heart bounded with relief at the knowledge that he'd left Loch Ness. Lord Rothlan, who was standing beside her, noticed her blinking back her tears.

"You are fond of your dragon, milady?" he asked.

"Yes, very," she answered.

He tightened his lips and turned her to face him. "Your father and I are at war, Lady Ellan. Your dragon is a fearsome weapon and you must know that I have no choice but to attack him."

She turned pale for although he looked impressive, she knew how harmless Arthur really was.

"And your Amgarad! Are you not fond of him?" she countered. His chin lifted but the strained, blank look that crossed his face told her all that she wanted to know.

"Where *are* your eagles?" she queried. "May I know?"

"They are on the border," he answered shortly and, turning from her abruptly, fixed his eyes on Arthur who was now soaring across the loch towards them. There was an awed hush among the defenders as he swooped on the castle.

A sharp order broke the silence and seconds later Rothlan's archers sent up a hail of arrows that bounced harmlessly off the dragon's scaly skin. Rothlan then raised his arm and great balls of fire shot into the air from cannons on the battlements. With a flap of his wings, Arthur avoided them deftly and, for the first time, Ellan noticed that Archie was perched on Arthur's back.

Unlike Arthur, Archie was vulnerable. The archers took advantage of this and promptly sent salvo after salvo of arrows shafting towards him. Tactically, however, it was a mistake, as Arthur was not amused at this attempt to kill his friend. Indeed, nothing was better calculated to rouse his wrath. His whole body erupted with rage as his temper flared. Now dragons are pretty fearsome beasts at the best of times but bad-tempered dragons really take the biscuit. He let out a roar that considerably startled Lady Ellan who, quite frankly, did not think he had it in him. But Arthur had grown up and now a proper dragon, proceeded to create merry hell round the walls of the castle.

Rothlan's men retaliated by firing more flaming cannon balls and there was a cheer from the defenders as one grazed his side. Arthur roared again, made a tight turn that nearly sent Archie into the loch, and swooping over the archers sent a stream of fire licking over them that emptied that particular section of the battlements in ten seconds flat. He then proceeded to roar furiously round the castle, breathing fire everywhere. Looking up, Rothlan saw Amgarad's nest go up in flames and as the dragon swept close to them, he grasped Lady Ellan's hand and pulled her to the safety of one of the guard houses.

Archie, however, caught sight of the green flash of her dress and yelled at Arthur. "Lady Ellan is there, with Rothlan. I saw them!"

Arthur veered out over the loch to turn again towards the castle when the archers let off another salvo of arrows. From the window of the guardhouse turret,

Ellan saw Archie fall forward on Arthur's back. As she cried out in horror, Rothlan strode to the window and chanted the words of a spell; a powerful spell invoking terrible forces, that would, however, drive her precious dragon from the skies and save him from further harm.

The flash of lightning that streaked from the turret window almost cracked the walls of the castle and, jagging across the water to the distant hills, lifted the waters of the loch in vicious waves. As the lightning sheered into the sky there was such a huge rumble of thunder that Archie, feverishly clutching the arrow that pierced his arm, thought it would never stop. "For goodness sake, Arthur, land somewhere safe," he groaned. "It looks as though Rothlan's called up the storm carriers! Good Lord! Just look at them!"

The storm carriers were a fearsome sight as they strode the heavens, wreaking havoc where they trod. Jarishan Castle stood black against the lightning flashes, its turrets shook under the roar of the thunder and its windows groaned in protest as the rain that streaked from the sky, lashed them in fury. The storm carriers moved over the mountains, carrying their handiwork to the borders of Jarishan where the MacArthur's army heard their approach and looked wonderingly at a sky that suddenly lowered in hues of crimson and purple-black.

"The storm carriers!" the MacArthur snarled. "He's released them against us!"

Sir James could only gape at them in wonder. Illustrations from children's tales flew through his mind as he gazed in awe at the rich reds, blues, yellows and greens of their fabulous, jewelled costumes; for the storm carriers were mystical, magical creatures. Their bearded faces were dark against the livid colours of their bright turbans and silk-striped robes as they whipped and lashed the storm to a frenzy of fury and noise.

"MacArthur!" he shouted against the howl of the wind that suddenly shrieked around them. "What on earth are they?"

"They are not of the earth," answered the MacArthur, "they are of the sky and while they're around we can't use the carpets for they are not invisible to them! We'll have to go to the castle on foot."

Sir James, who was not as fit as he would have liked, looked apprehensively at the driving rain that was fast turning to sleet and wondered if he would make it. The MacArthur, however, read his thoughts and put a hand on his arm. "Don't worry, Sir James! You'll make it! The firestones will protect you and give you the strength you need; for although it is not many miles to Jarishan, it will be hard going in this weather. Wrap up well, take your carpet and use your furs to protect you from the cold, for the storm carriers will do everything in their power to stop us from reaching the loch."

It was when the sleet turned to snow and they were well into Jarishan that Sir James remembered Neil and Clara. They must be with their father, he thought, as he concentrated on putting his feet on firm ground rather than the deceptively smooth patches of snow that lured the unwary into deep drifts.

But neither Neil nor Clara was with their father. Nor were they together. Neil's carpet had crossed into Jarishan in the split second that Arthur had broken through its protective shield and although he had shouted to Archie as they made their way across the mountain, he had been unable to attract his attention. His carpet, however, seemed quite happy to follow the dragon and it was only when Arthur headed across the loch that Neil brought his carpet down by the water's edge and had a grandstand view of Arthur's attack on Jarishan Castle.

When he saw that Archie had been wounded, he leapt up, flung himself on his carpet and was already half-way across the loch when the whole world seemed to erupt around him as Rothlan summoned the storm carriers to do his bidding. Neil ducked as a lightning bolt streaked over his head and his carpet bucked like a startled horse as the waves beneath them suddenly became mountains of black, frothing water. As he sped towards Arthur and Archie, who had landed at the far end of the island, he had a spectacular view of the storm carriers as they flung themselves round the castle and spread havoc over loch and mountain. It was a storm to end all storms, thought Neil in awe.

Thankfully, he put his carpet down beside Arthur and materialized before a white-faced Archie who lay propped against the dragon's side. Archie looked up at him in amazement, his hair plastered over his face by the driving rain. A worried Arthur hissed in relief as Neil appeared.

"Neil!" the dragon cried, "thank goodness you have come! Archie is injured!"

"Am I pleased to see *you!*" Archie grinned feebly. "It's pretty painful but I think I'll be all right!"

Neil bent over him and quickly examined the wound. Although it was jagged and nasty, there seemed to be little bleeding. "He'll be all right, Arthur," Neil told the worried dragon.

"Nothing to worry about, I'll be okay!" Archie muttered. "It's just a flesh wound."

"You're right," said Neil who, although he'd never seen a flesh wound before, thought that it looked clean enough. "We must find some shelter, though. You're soaking wet."

Archie struggled to his feet and holding his arm awkwardly because of the arrow, looked round. "We must get off the island or we'll be captured. There seems to

be a boathouse over there on the shore. Can you see it?
To the left of that stand of trees! It looks big enough to
hold Arthur and he won't mind being in the water."

"Can you manage on Arthur's back, though?" questioned Neil worriedly. "There's the devil of a gale blowing
out there!"

"I'll use your carpet, Neil. It'll be safer. That is, if
you don't mind going over on Arthur's back?"

Neil gulped. "No, no," he stammered. "I wouldn't
mind at all! I'd enjoy it, really!"

Archie sat down on the soaking carpet and disappeared as Neil hesitantly approached Arthur.

"Climb onto his wing first and then get on his back,"
instructed Archie's disembodied voice.

Arthur lowered his wing obligingly and Neil, his
heart pounding with excitement, clambered onto it.
Despite the relentless rain, Arthur's skin was bone
dry. The water poured off him in streams. Neil's train-
ers, therefore, got a good grip on his scales and with a
final scramble he managed to perch on Arthur's back,
just behind his neck. He was so excited that he could
barely speak but hugged Arthur and shouted that he
was ready to go. He didn't see the carpet take off but
knew that it must have done so when Arthur flapped
his wings and rose effortlessly into the air.

It was a ride that Neil was never to forget. He had
not, until then, appreciated the sheer power of the dragon's muscles as his great wings powered it through the
storm. He hung on to Arthur's neck as the full weight of
the wind and rain blasted him as they moved out over
the loch and fervently hoped that Archie would be all
right, although he knew that the carpet would protect
him. All too soon, however, the outline of the decrepit
boathouse loomed out of the rain and to his relief Neil
saw that Archie was already waiting for them.

"How did it go?" asked Archie.

"It was marvellous!" Neil answered, slipping down onto Arthur's wing and jumping to the ground. "Fabulous! I'll never forget it!" He turned and hugged Arthur ecstatically. "I just can't believe that I've actually flown on a dragon!"

"Now that we're here, we'd better get Arthur inside before anyone spots him," urged Archie, who was looking strained and white.

Neil opened the ramshackle door into the boathouse. It smelt stale and musty inside but no boats were moored alongside the rickety platform that stretched along one side of the building. Walking to the far end, he managed to push open the double doors that gave onto the loch and Arthur gave him the fright of his life as he poked his huge head in from the other side to inspect his new quarters.

"Will you fit in, Arthur, do you think?"

Arthur grunted and crawled in, for the water was shallow. When, however, he discovered that he didn't have room to turn round, he went out again and backed in, so that the double doors faced him. It was only then that Neil appreciated how big Arthur actually was, as his great bulk more or less filled the narrow confines of the boathouse. It was a cold, wet place and Neil shivered instinctively as he helped Archie settle on a pile of old nets. Neil's waterproof jacket had protected him against the worst ravages of the storm and he was relatively dry in comparison to Archie, who was soaked to the skin and shivering violently. Neil used a boathook to tear the sleeve of Archie's tunic so that he could remove the sopping garment without too much bother.

"Hang my clothes at the end of the boat-hook, Neil," instructed Archie, "so that Arthur can dry them."

"So that Arthur can dry them?" repeated Neil stupidly.

"He's a dragon, remember!"

Neil gulped, looking warily at Arthur who was watching them from the water. He didn't seem too comfortable and kept sniffing the air worriedly. Neil sympathized. The storm giants were enough to upset anyone.

"Is that wise?" he asked Archie doubtfully. "This place is made of wood. It'll go up in smoke if it catches fire."

"You'll be careful, Arthur, won't you?"

Arthur started. He seemed about to speak but thought better of it when he looked at Archie's arm. Obediently he turned towards them and started to blow little puffs of flame that certainly didn't seem to be doing any harm. Neil not only managed to dry Archie's clothes but took off his own jeans and dried them like toast on the end of the boat-hook. Even the magic carpet managed to dry out and by the time the laundry was done, the boathouse was warm and comfortable. Neil propped himself exhaustedly against the wall and worried. He worried about the MacArthurs, about Archie and the arrow, which he was sure should be removed, and about Clara. Thank goodness he had spoken to Clara before he had broken through the shield. At least he knew that she was safe! Arthur continued to blow little bursts of fire from time to time and after the hurly-burly of the storm, the pleasant warmth of the boathouse was insensibly soothing. It was not long before he and Archie closed their eyes and fell fast asleep.

Arthur looked at them with satisfaction and, gently heaving his bulk through the double doors of the boathouse, slipped unseen into the stormy waters of Loch Jarishan.

28. Clara's Adventure

Neil had soothed himself with the knowledge that Clara was safe. Had he but known it, however, this was not the case. Clara was by no means safe. She was in the middle of the storm on her carpet.

This was not actually her doing. She had been standing on her own, idly watching the MacArthur and Sir James talking, when her carpet had floated quietly up behind her and banged its edge against the back of her legs with such force that she had toppled back onto it. Before she could say anything, it had shot off. As she had become invisible the minute she had landed on it, no one had noticed her somewhat unorthodox departure and as her father, Sir James and Dougal had become separated on the ground, each thought that the other was looking after her.

Now that the protective shield had been broken, Clara's carpet sped over Jarishan faster than she had ever flown before. The carpet however, hadn't reckoned on the storm and as the black and purple clouds rolled towards them, it dived to hug the ground. But the storm carriers had spotted it and reached out their giant hands to grasp Clara and dash her to the ground. The carpet knew her danger and swerved this way and that to keep her out of their way. Indeed, Clara only managed to stay on board by looping her wrists through its fringe so that she was virtually tied to it.

"Use your firestone, Clara," a voice said urgently. "Use your firestone! It will protect you from the storm carriers!" Clara looked around in amazement. She couldn't think where the voice was coming from. Then, as her carpet side-slipped frantically, the voice spoke again in a gasping whisper. "Hurry, Clara, I can't keep this up much longer!"

It was then that Clara realized that her carpet was talking to here. In desperation, she freed one hand and fished the firestone out of her pocket with the other. Shaking with fear, she held it in the turbaned faces of the giants. Ellan had given her a particularly beautiful stone and its magic was strong, as Clara herself had taken it fresh from the eyes of the dragon. The storm carriers paused in their vicious attack and although they did not disappear, they eased away and although still buffeted by wind and rain, the carpet now flew on unmolested. With a huge sigh of relief, Clara tucked the firestone away again and, moving herself into the middle of the carpet, sat upright. Shivering with cold, for she had lost all her furs, she peered over the edge of the carpet to see where she was.

Her eyes searched the gusting waves of snow that blew round her and once she thought she could vaguely see the peaks of mountains far below. The carpet did not speak to her again, and, although she trusted it, she wondered why it had brought her on such a perilous venture. But only when it lost height and the snow gave way to driving rain did she finally understand. In front of her, through its opaque curtain, she could see an island in the middle of a loch. On it stood a most beautiful castle. Jarishan Castle! The carpet had brought her to Lady Ellan!

The loch was still stormy and great waves crashed against the island but the mountains now lay between Jarishan and the storm carriers and, as she looked back over her shoulder, she felt pity for the MacArthur and his troops who must be bearing the brunt of their attack.

The carpet now edged its way round the castle walls, looking for a way in. An unfastened door on the roof, banging in the wind, gave it access and once inside the building it floated along passages and down stone staircases. At one stage, Clara's heart jumped to her throat when she heard someone coming up the stairs. The carpet soared towards the ceiling and pressed Clara flat against it as the man passed underneath them with inches to spare.

Then Clara heard Ellan's voice behind a thick door. The door was shut but the carpet floated near the handle so that Clara could gently turn it. Ellan was inside the room and, by the sound of it, was having an argument with Lord Rothlan.

As the door opened, a gust of cold air blew into the room and Rothlan, who had been standing by the fire, walked over and closed it. His face was thoughtful as he returned to his stance by the mantelpiece.

"You were saying, milady?"

Ellan gathered her thoughts together quickly, for while Rothlan had gone to close the door, Clara had reached out and gripped her arm briefly.

"I have been trying to tell you for the past ten minutes that all this is totally unnecessary!"

"I told you, Lady Ellan," he said curtly. "I will fight to keep the firestones. My position hasn't altered. If you will not give them to me, then you will have to stay here."

"If you fight my father then we will both be weakened. Kalman will rub his hands with glee when he finds out that we are at war! You are playing into his hands, can't you see that?"

Rothlan eyed her consideringly. "You are right, I suppose ... but ... excuse me for a moment. I have something to attend to." He bowed and left the room.

As the door closed, Clara leapt off her carpet and ran to Lady Ellan. "Lady Ellan! Are you alright? Has he hurt you?"

"Of course not, Clara," she hugged her warmly despite her wet, bedraggled appearance. "Rothlan is a gentleman. I have nothing to fear while I am here."

"The carpet brought me to you. You must use it to escape!" She looked at it doubtfully. "It's not really big enough for two. I'll stay here if it can't carry us both."

Lady Ellan hugged Clara again. "Dear Clara, you are a loyal friend indeed." She turned and looked at the carpet. "Come here," she said smiling, and Clara watched as it flew to her happily.

"The reason I gave you this carpet, Clara, and the reason it brought you here is because it was my carpet when I was your age. It must have been worried about me and thought it would try to rescue me." She rubbed a hand gently over its silky pile and smiled as the carpet fluttered and rippled in response. "We had such good times together, but I can't use it to leave Jarishan, Clara. I've given my word to Lord Rothlan that I will not try to escape and I must keep my word."

"I agree," nodded Clara, "you must keep your word. But Ellan, your father and his army will be here to rescue you soon. Arthur cried buckets of tears when he came back from Loch Ness and the shield around Jarishan has been broken already."

"How very interesting!" said a soft voice from the door. Rothlan entered the room, closing the door behind him. "I wasn't born yesterday," he snapped as he saw the surprised look on their faces. "But I am glad, Lady Ellan, that you would not break your word to me."

She watched him thoughtfully as he bowed to Clara. "The little lady of the café," he murmured. "I'm pleased to meet you!"

Clara curtseyed awkwardly and shook his hand. He gestured to chairs near the fire and put more logs on before he, too, drew up a chair and sat facing them.

"May I make a suggestion, Lord Rothlan?"

"By all means, Lady Ellan."

"Clara has just told me that my father now has many firestones. This means that we no longer need to rely on the ones I'm wearing."

"So you will give them to me?"

"I'll give them to you if my father approves. He is marching overland with his army and will reach the shores of the loch soon, according to Clara. Perhaps you could call off the storm carriers and invite him here to talk the matter over. Clara could take the letter." She looked at Clara who nodded in agreement.

Rothlan bit his lip as he thought the matter over. "Very well," he said abruptly, "stay here while I write the letter. I'll have some tea sent while you are waiting."

Hector Mackenzie's wife brought the tea on a huge silver tray and laid it out for them on a side table. Clara eyed the plates of sandwiches and scones appreciatively for she was very hungry and still suffering from the ordeal of her journey.

"Gracious me, dearie," Mrs MacKenzie fussed. "And what have you been up to? You're as white as a sheet! And look at your hair! Soaking wet!" And she fussed away to bring a towel.

The magic carpet, which had been gradually creeping closer to the warmth of the fire while Mrs Mackenzie had been laying out the tea, froze in its tracks as it heard her remarks. Clara saw it stop out of the corner of her eye and turned to Lady Ellan. "The storm carriers were really scary," she said, "but the carpet told me to use my firestone against them and they left us alone." She shook her head. "I didn't know carpets could talk!"

Lady Ellan nodded. "They don't speak often but yes, they can talk when they have to. And they can understand what we say!" However, she looked suspiciously at the carpet, which, settling itself somewhat guiltily in front of the fire, started to steam gently.

By the time Lord Rothlan returned with his letter, Lady Ellan and Clara had enjoyed a satisfying tea and Clara had told her all about Dougal MacLeod and the story of Arthur's stay in Loch Ness.

Lady Ellan grimaced when she heard that Dougal MacLeod had now become one of them. "I owe him a tremendous apology," she sighed. "I don't know quite how I'm going to phrase it either." She gestured helplessly. "How does one apologize for a thing like that! Hamish and Jaikie were quite harsh with him, you know!"

"I shouldn't worry, Lady Ellan! When you get to know him, he's really quite nice!"

Lady Ellan walked to the window and looked out anxiously. "It's my father and his men that I'm really worried about! The storm carriers are fearsome creatures and it looks as though a blizzard is blowing over there. The mountains are white!"

Lord Rothlan heard the latter part of her remark as he entered the room. "I have already called off the storm carriers so that Clara can make her journey in safety," he informed them.

Clara curtseyed shyly as he held out a large cream envelope, its elaborate red seal embossed with the crest of a swooping eagle.

She traced it with her finger before looking up and meeting his stern gaze.

"Amgarad?" she whispered.

He almost smiled. "The crest of our clan has always been an eagle, Clara. Just as that of Lady Ellan," and here he turned and bowed to her formally, "bears a dragon."

Sensing that it was needed, Clara's carpet moved from the warmth of the fire and hovered beside her so that she could slip onto it easily. Lady Ellan moved forward and spread two furs on top of it.

"Wrap up warmly, Clara. It is still freezing in the mountains." She then caught the carpet by its fringe and pulled at it gently. "The way is clear for you to find my father, but no more daring adventures, my friend!" she warned. "But I am grateful to you for bringing Clara to me. It was well done! God speed and look after Clara!"

The carpet wilted slightly round the edges at her strictures and, satisfied that it was suitably chastened, Lady Ellan watched Clara as she climbed on, drew one of the furs around her, and disappeared. Lord Rothlan threw open a casement window so that she could leave and, as the carpet sailed through it, she called goodbye.

Rothlan quickly closed the window as a blast of freezing air surged into the room and as they looked out across the loch, Lady Ellan pointed out the eagles, circling in the sky.

"Your eagles seem to have weathered the storm well," she remarked.

He looked at them sharply. "Yes, I'd forgotten about them! Please excuse me, I must go to my crystal and call them in. They will attack your father and his men otherwise." He left her at the window, wondering idly how long it would take her father to arrive. Not long, if he used a carpet, she thought.

29. Amgarad's Agony

In the meantime, Clara's carpet zoomed happily across the loch. Although the waves still flashed white with foam, Clara could see that the storm had abated and would soon die out completely. Her carpet was flying fairly swiftly and she bent forward eagerly, trying to catch a glimpse of the MacArthur's army.

The sudden departure of the storm carriers had come as a relief to the MacArthur's men as they struggled through the blizzards and now able to use their carpets they had quickly made up for lost time. The summit of the mountain peaks now lay well behind them and it was only when the loch and castle of Jarishan appeared in front of them that the MacArthur called a halt and they gathered to make final plans.

Clara, still clutching Lord Rothlan's letter, was somewhat puzzled as her carpet dipped towards the ground so quickly. She had barely left the castle and could see nothing on the ground but snow and trees and it was only as the carpet prepared to land that she saw them clearly. There was no sign of Neil but Sir James, Dougal and her father were there, standing on a slight rise talking to the MacArthur. As she materialized in front of the MacArthur, there was a sudden stir and her father ran forward.

"Clara!" he exclaimed. "Where have you been? We've all been looking for you!"

"I've been with Lady Ellan, Dad," she said. "I'm fine and so is she." She then turned to the MacArthur and held out the letter. "Lord Rothlan gave me this letter for you."

They all looked at one another in amazement as the MacArthur broke the seal and glanced quickly over the contents. "Hmmmph!" he said. "He wants to talk, does he?"

Clara smiled. "I think Lady Ellan has been busy!"

So intent was everyone on Clara's sudden appearance that no one noticed the eagles swooping down from the skies. It was Dougal MacLeod who gave the warning.

"The eagles!" he shouted, "Look out!"

Amgarad, wings pulled back and talons outstretched, was a fearsome sight. Well in front of the rest of the eagles, he was heading straight for the MacArthur and, seeing that he had been spotted, let out a dreadful cry that froze the blood.

The MacArthur looked up and saw him dropping like a stone towards him. He dropped Rothlan's letter and his hand instinctively straightened to cast a spell. The soldiers cheered as a streak of light flew from his fingers to hex the evil bird.

Amgarad didn't stand a chance. The ray of light caught and held him in its beam for a brief instant before exploding with a vicious crack and, caught in mid-flight, the dreadful bird blew up in a shower of dirty, ragged feathers.

Clara was appalled. "MacArthur!" she cried as the other eagles screamed wildly out of harm's way and scattered across the sky. "MacArthur! What have you done?"

"It's for the best," growled the MacArthur grumpily as Amgarad's body hit the ground with a thump.

Clara turned to see if he were really dead. Perhaps, she thought, he might only be injured. Let him just be injured, she prayed, for Ellan had told her that Rothlan adored the bird. Fearfully, she moved forward to where he lay on the ground, frighteningly still amid the drift of fluff and feathers that still dropped gently from the sky.

As she approached, however, Amgarad moved jerkily and sat up. As he staggered to his feet, Clara stopped and stared at him in disbelief. Amgarad was not dead; he was very much alive. But her eyes rounded in horror at the enormity of his plight.

For Amgarad had no feathers! He stood there in the snow, a pathetic sight with a body like a plucked chicken. As he realized what had happened to him, he looked up and met her eyes with an expression of such abject shame and misery that she felt like bursting into tears. Shivering violently and trying to cover his nakedness with stubbly wings, he cringed before her in complete humiliation.

Clara ran to him, snatching one of the furs from her carpet as she went. Quickly she wrapped it round him before anyone else saw his disgrace. She was furious with the MacArthur! How could he? How could he? Carrying Amgarad, she jumped on her carpet. "Take me to Lady Ellan!" she snapped.

Ellan had watched the eagles swooping out of the sky with some anxiety and breathed a sigh of relief as she saw them abort their attack. Thank goodness, she thought, as she watched them scatter across the sky, Rothlan must have managed to get through to them in the nick of time. But where was Amgarad? Her eyes searched the sky frantically.

Rothlan came in and stood beside her. It was his first question. "Where is Amgarad?" he asked, watching the eagles as they winged their way back to the castle.

"Didn't you speak to him?"

"No, the crystal remained dull. Excuse me, I must go upstairs to find out what has happened."

Rothlan almost ran out of the room and Ellan, after a final glance over the waters of the loch, followed him apprehensively. By the time she reached the battlements, the birds were already perched round him and, pausing at the top of the stairs, she saw from his stance that the news had not been good.

Grimly she moved towards him over the old stone flags of the upper reaches of the castle. Although the dreadful birds flopped and hopped out of her way as she approached, they crowded in behind her, croaking and hissing venomously. She touched Rothlan lightly on the arm and he struggled for composure as he turned to face her.

"Amgarad is dead," he said dully, his face set. "Your father hexed him."

The cluster of foul-looking birds closed in threateningly; screaming and hissing with anger, many had their cruel heads poised to strike. She stood her ground and looked at him uncertainly. Did he plan to feed her to his birds? He must have read her thoughts, however, for he waved them back and once more turned to the battlements to gaze across the loch.

Ellan followed his gaze and saw her father's army at the edge of the water.

"I will fight," he said stonily, "to avenge Amgarad's death, if nothing else."

"Lord Rothlan," she said nervously, pleating the folds of her dress in anxious hands, "I know things look black but I also know my father. He would never kill Amgarad."

"The eagles say that he did and they were there."

"I still don't believe it!" she asserted defiantly.

It was at this moment that Clara materialized from her carpet, clutching a fur-clad bundle that rested, strangely still, in her arms. The eagles flapped their

wings warningly and Rothlan and Ellan swung round
to see what had so disturbed them.

"Clara!" Ellan gasped. For Clara's eyes were stream-
ing with tears.

"Can ... can we go downstairs?" Clara choked. "It's
all right, Lord Rothlan," she said, seeing his face,
"Amgarad is alive!"

"Alive!" Rothlan's face lit up as he shed a weight
that had been almost too much to bear. "Is he injured?"
Rothlan strode forward to take him from Clara's hands.
"Let me see what happened to him!"

"No, no, not here!" Clara cried desperately as the
other birds surged eagerly forward.

Her words came too late, however. Rothlan grasped
him from her arms and the fur fell to the ground.
Amgarad perched on Rothlan's arm for all the world
to see.

Clara stared at him in amazement, Rothlan nearly
dropped him and Lady Ellan looked at him with dawn-
ing understanding. For Amgarad was not the naked,
pimpled bird that Clara had gathered in her arms a
mere ten minutes before, nor was he the foul, evil-
looking monster that had attacked her at the well in
Holyrood Park.

Amgarad was an eagle — a fabulous, glorious eagle.

Amgarad, it seemed, could not quite believe his
good fortune either. He stretched one talon and then
the other, examining his sleek feathered legs. He then
looked down at his chest, stretched his great wings and
finally realized just what had happened. His black eyes
glistened with happiness and the call that rang out
from the battlements was not the dreadful cry of the
bird he had been, but the pure call of the eagle.

Clara went to pieces, she was so happy. Shaking with
emotion, she sobbed her heart out in Lady Ellan's arms

and did not see Rothlan's delight as Amgarad flew from his arm and circled the battlements triumphantly.

"Father!" Lady Ellan blinked as the MacArthur materialized from his carpet, followed by some of his men.

Clara turned away, rubbing her eyes, as Lady Ellan moved forward to greet her father. The MacArthur then strode towards Rothlan, hand outstretched. Rothlan stepped forward and took it.

"Well, Alasdair!" said the MacArthur, "nice to see you again. How's the fishing these days?"

Rothlan's eyes gleamed in amusement. "Pretty good," was his reply, "the rivers are full of trout."

"And do ye still have that rascal of a ghillie? Whit was his name?"

"Ye'll be meaning auld Duncan!" interrupted Hector Mackenzie, who had just arrived on the battlements.

"Hector Mackenzie!" the MacArthur shook his hand vigorously. "Ye havena changed a bit! There's something I was aye minded to ask you ..."

Amgarad, resplendent in his new feathers, swooped to perch on his master's shoulder as, deep in conversation Rothlan, the MacArthur and the rest of the men made their way through the narrow door that took them down to the main reception rooms of the castle.

Clara and Lady Ellan looked at one another and burst out laughing. "Isn't that just typical!" Ellan remarked. "Get them started on the fishing and you can't get a word in edgeways!"

30. Dragonsleep

Lady Ellan and Clara were just about to follow the men downstairs when Jaikie and Hamish materialized on the battlements.

"Lady Ellan!" Jaikie called, running over to her.

"Jaikie!" she smiled delightedly. "And Hamish! How nice it is to see you both. But tell me, how is Archie? I hope he wasn't badly hurt?"

"Archie! Hurt?" Hamish said in a horrified voice. "I didn't know that! When did it happen?"

"Why, when Arthur attacked the castle! Archie was hit by an arrow."

"Hit by an arrow?"

"Didn't Arthur fly back to you? It was just before Rothlan called up the storm carriers."

"Jaikie," questioned Clara, suddenly afraid. "Neil *is* with you, isn't he? I haven't seen him since we left Arthur's Seat."

Jaikie and Hamish looked at one another and Hamish shook his head.

"We haven't seen him since we left Edinburgh either," he confessed. "I thought he was with you!"

"Where on earth can he be?" whispered Clara.

"Do you think he might have been injured when we hit the shield," hazarded Jaikie. "He ... he might have fallen off his carpet and be lying injured somewhere."

"No, no, he wasn't injured," Clara was quite sure of that. "He was fine; he shouted to me to see if I was all right but his voice sounded far away. He wanted my carpet to fly closer to him."

"He might have broken through the shield with Arthur," ventured Hamish.

"If they are all missing then they are probably still together," said Ellan. "Remember, I was only able to see Arthur and Archie. Neil would be invisible on his carpet."

"We'll get a search party together. What do you think, Jaikie?"

Jaikie nodded. "You tell the MacArthur and I'll get the men organized."

A far off shout from the shore sent them to the battlements. At the edge of the loch, soldiers were swarming round a dilapidated boathouse.

"Carpet!" snapped Jaikie, clapping his hands. "Something's happening over there! Let's go!"

As if sensing their urgency, the carpets took them over the loch at a tearing speed that brought tears to Clara's eyes. Jumping off, they ran towards the boathouse where an officer greeted them with relief.

"It's Archie and the boy, Neil! They were in the boathouse when we went to check it over. The thing is, sir, we can't wake them up!"

"They're not ... not ...?" Clara couldn't utter the words.

"No, Miss Clara," the soldier assured her, "just asleep!"

The soldiers guarding the boathouse parted to let them through and in its damp recesses they saw Archie and Neil lying fast asleep. Clara gasped and put her hand over her mouth at the sight of the arrow that pierced Archie's arm.

Hamish and Jaikie looked at one another grimly as Ellan bent over them and put a hand on their foreheads. "Dragonsleep!" she pronounced.

Hamish gestured to the officer. "Have them taken to the castle!" he ordered.

"Dragonsleep!" echoed Clara, as some soldiers entered and lifted the still bodies onto stretchers. "What does that mean? Will they be all right?"

"Arthur has the power to send people to sleep. It depends on how long he's put them out for!" Ellan looked at them considering. "Personally I'd say it'll be some time yet before they wake up."

"They'll be all right. Don't worry about that," Jaikie assured her, seeing that Clara still looked alarmed. "It's Arthur that won't be all right, for when I get my hands on that dragon I'll ... I'll ...!" He waved his hands in the air, unable to decide on a suitable fate for Arthur.

"Give over, Jaikie!" snapped Hamish, "We're wasting time! Let's try and work out what must have happened!"

"Well, Arthur was here for a start," said Clara, sniffing the air. "I can smell his smell."

"Yes, yes, he must have been here. But where has he gone? And why would he put them to sleep and leave them?"

"Especially as Archie was wounded," agreed Clara.

"They probably came here to shelter from the storm. I doubt if they'd take on the storm carriers," decided Ellan.

"But why would Arthur leave them? Archie was wounded. Arthur would rather die than leave him."

"It must have been something very important then," said Clara seriously. "And something he didn't want to tell them about. Something he wanted to do on his own. I bet he put them to sleep because he didn't want them to know where he was going."

"But where did he go?"

"Did you see him again, milady, after Archie was hit?"

Lady Ellan shook her head. "The storm carriers were all over the place. He couldn't have flown anywhere. Even dragons don't argue with storm carriers."

"Clara," said Hamish in a strange voice. "What did you say when we first came in here?"

"I asked if they'd be all right?"

"After that! Think! About Arthur. You said you knew he'd been here."

"Well, yes," said Clara. "I can smell him, can't you?"

"There is a musty smell in here," said Lady Ellan, sniffing the air. "But surely it's just the dampness of the boathouse?"

"It's not Arthur," Jaikie said positively. "Dragons don't have a smell."

Clara looked mutinous. "Yes, they do," she asserted. "Maybe you have just grown used to it but when he came back from Loch Ness I noticed it." She wrinkled her nose. "A funny, musty smell."

"Water goblins!" whispered Hamish, appalled.

Lady Ellan paled. "Water goblins!" she repeated. "Hamish, are you sure?"

"Water goblins!" Jaikie was astounded. "But what would they be doing here?"

"I don't know, but maybe Lord Rothlan can tell us!" Hamish ground out. "One thing's for sure! Arthur didn't take to the skies, milady. He took to the loch!"

They ran back to their carpets and in minutes were back on the island where they found Lord Rothlan and the MacArthur in one of the bedrooms reassuring the Ranger that Neil would wake up naturally in a few hours. Hector Mackenzie was bending over a second bed, tying a bandage round Archie's arm.

"Clean wound!" he said cheerfully, "but just as well to take the arrow out while he's still asleep. He'll be as right as rain in ... no ... time!" His voice tailed off as he saw the expression on Hamish's face.

"What's happened now?" Lord Rothlan asked sharply.

"It's something that I think we should discuss together, if it please you, milord."

"Certainly," Rothlan looked puzzled. "We can leave Neil and Archie to sleep, now that they have been made comfortable. Shall we go downstairs?"

He led them into a large room furnished with comfortable armchairs. Servants were carrying in heavy trays of food and he motioned them to be seated.

"This won't wait!" said Hamish as the servants left the room. "Sorry, Lord Rothlan, but we have just discovered that Arthur was in the boathouse with Neil and Archie and it stank of water goblins! We believe that he's gone into the loch after them!"

"*Water goblins!*" came the astounded reply. "In *my* loch!" Lord Rothlan's voice was incredulous. "You *must* be joking! Are you *sure?*"

"Pretty sure!" confirmed Jaikie.

Lord Rothlan flung out his hands helplessly and looked at Lady Ellan. "Water goblins!" he said. "You mentioned Kalman and the water goblins! But why? It's beyond me! Why on earth would water goblins come to Jarishan?"

"If there are water goblins in the loch," stated the MacArthur, "then they will have come for a reason! But what could it be? What is there in your loch, Alasdair, that they would want?"

"Apart from the fish, I've truly no idea!"

"Well, they've either been there for ages or they've just arrived," Dougal MacLeod stated, "for the shield around Jarishan couldn't be broken, could it!"

Lord Rothlan nodded in agreement and then stiffened. "What a fool I've been," he muttered. "What – a – fool!"

"Calm yourself, Alasdair," said the MacArthur, "one thing you were never was a fool!"

Rothlan rose to his feet and started to pace the room. "I got it all the wrong way round from the beginning," he said bitterly. He stopped and throwing out his hands, turned to face them. "I thought that by giving me the power to break the shield, the crystal was giving me a way to free Jarishan. But that was not actually the point of the exercise at all! Fool that I was! Kalman's been searching all the lochs around here and had to break the shield to get into mine as well!"

"But what do you have in your loch that is so vital?" Sir James asked.

"No stories of Spanish gold and buried treasure?" queried MacLeod.

Rothlan's eyes flew to those of the MacArthur. "I don't know what he could be looking for, unless ... There is ..." he said hesitantly, "... it's an old story, but you must have heard it MacArthur."

"The Sultan's Crown?"

Rothlan nodded. "Legend has always had it that it was lost in this area. I don't quite know what to think." He shook his head doubtfully. "It couldn't be, could it?"

"Arthur told Neil and me that the water goblins were searching at the bottom of Loch Ness for buried treasure," said Clara hesitantly. "Nessie told him that Prince Kalman had asked the chief of the water goblins to search all the lochs."

"Kalman, eh? That would explain a lot!" muttered the MacArthur grimly.

"Loch Ness! But it's miles away!" Hamish said.

"Still within the general area though," Lady Ellan said thoughtfully. "Perhaps Kalman has a list of likely places to search ... and, believe me, it is only someone as ruthless as him who would be so thorough in his search! Even if it weren't in Loch Jarishan, he'd want to score it off his list!"

"What's the story behind the Sultan's Crown?" asked the Ranger.

"You tell the tale, Alasdair," nodded the MacArthur. "It's so old that I've forgotten the half of it!"

"The Sultan's Crown was a faery crown that belonged, in years gone by, to Sulaiman the Red, the Ottoman Sultan of Turkey. Many faeries used to visit Turkey because it was there that the finest magic carpets could be bought. In those days, Kalman's father, Prince Casimir, was the most powerful of the Scottish Lords of the North but his power was nothing compared to that of the Osmanli, the Turks. Everyone knew that the Sultan's power totally outshone his. His jealousy consumed him and over the years he became obsessed with the thought of owning the crown, which was the root of Ottoman power. He couldn't buy it, for it wasn't for sale and he couldn't steal it as it was too well protected so he challenged the Turkish Sultan to a contest. Whoever's magic proved the stronger would win the crown.

"No one expected the Sultan to lose, but lose he did and he had to hand over the crown of his own free will. Prince Casimir had already taken the crown and was on his way back to Scotland when it was discovered that he had cheated and in his fury the Turkish Sultan sent the storm carriers to bring the crown back. However, the storm carriers conjured up such a dreadful storm that, at some stage in the journey, the crown fell off the magic carpet and landed, it is said, somewhere on the west coast of Scotland.

"Although faeries have searched for it for centuries it has never been found but in Turkey its loss was felt almost at once. No more magic carpets were ever made and over the years, the great Turkish Empire waned. The Sultan never forgave us and there has been bad blood between the faeries of Scotland and the Osmanli ever since."

"And Prince Casimir?" asked Sir James.

Rothlan looked at him and smiled wryly. "No one knows what happened to him. Perhaps the storm carriers finished him off. His carpet was found in shreds somewhere in Sutherland but his body was never found."

"Of course! The carpet! That must be it!" Lady Ellan said suddenly, sitting up straight in her chair. "It must be! Old Agnes!"

They looked at her blankly.

"Agnes," she said, turning to her father. "I told you, she disappeared for months on end and turned up muttering weird stories of goblins and a magic forest. Nobody really paid much attention to her ramblings but if I remember rightly, the black tower of Ardray is surrounded by a magic forest and I've heard tell of goblins in its woods."

"Agnes? Who's she?" asked Sir James.

"Agnes is a carpet mender. She's as old as the hills and spends her time going round all the castles and estates, mending their magic carpets. In fact, she's been around so long that she knows them all by name!" She looked at her father grimly and said in an altered tone. "Father — what if she *was* in Ardray and what if the carpet she was asked to mend was Prince Casimir's carpet?"

Rothlan sprang to his feet. "If Agnes managed to put *that* carpet together again, it would tell Kalman everything!" he said, appalled. "What happened when the storm carriers attacked his father! Where the crown fell! It would tell him everything he wanted to know!"

"And if Kalman finds the Sultan's Crown?" asked Sir James.

There was a bleak silence.

"It's magic is such that he would rule us all."

"And not," said the MacArthur getting to his feet, "for the better! Now Alasdair! If we are all going to be digging around in the mud at the bottom of your loch for a crown that may or may not be there, to say nothing of fending off water goblins at the same time, then I, for one, want a decent meal inside me before we begin!"

31. Battle of the Giants

It was, nevertheless, several hours before they were able to start. After a brief discussion, they decided that the only way to investigate what was going on in the loch was to merge with the fish. Although Dougal MacLeod looked understandably doubtful at the prospect he had no intention of missing out on such an adventure and, with the others, threw himself whole-heartedly into the preparations.

Rothlan's men hurriedly took boats out onto the loch to net some fish and it was not long before Hector arrived to tell them that enough had been caught for their purpose.

From the beginning, Lady Ellan and Clara were told quite forcefully that there was no way that they would be allowed to participate in the venture. The MacArthur put it bluntly. "Ye're no' coming," he stated flatly. "It's far too dangerous and besides, Archie and Neil will soon be waking up and they'll need you to look after them." And that, it would seem, was that!

The sun was still high in the sky as they all moved down to the shore. Above them, the eagles wheeled and swooped, revelling in their new feathers, for the MacArthur had lifted the spell that had bound them for so many years. Jarishan, too, had been freed from its enchantment as, after lunch, Lady Ellan had presented the set of firestones to Lord Rothlan.

Their influence, thought Clara, was already pervading the castle and bringing to it an indefinable sense of ease and contentment. A warm breeze whispered along the side of the loch as she walked by the shore and listened to the murmur of the waves. Such a peaceful place, she thought. If only there were no water goblins to spoil it all. She watched Amgarad sweep down from the sky and perch on Rothlan's shoulder. Amgarad, she could see, was not at all happy at what was going on in the loch and would, she knew, be devastated if anything were to happen to his master. She heaved a huge sigh and walked towards the jetty where the little group had gathered to merge with the fish. The MacArthur pointed out the fat trout that awaited them.

"You'll see that they have a small gold ring piercing the sides of their mouths," he said. "That way we'll be able to recognise one another in the water."

Hector, Hamish and Jaikie went first and with a wave to the others, disappeared. The MacArthur looked squarely at Sir James, the Ranger and MacLeod. "Er ... you're all quite sure about this, are you?" His gaze encompassed the three of them. "I'm not forcing you to go, you know that, don't you?"

"We wouldn't miss it for the world," Sir James assured him, stepping forward. He paused and turned to wave to Clara and Ellan before grasping one of the trout in both hands and merging with it swiftly. MacLeod and the Ranger who had followed him into the water, did the same. The Ranger had already hugged Clara and told her to look after her brother but, watching him disappear into the loch brought hot tears to her eyes and she turned away to hide them.

The MacArthur turned to Ellan and hugged her. Holding her at arm's length he spoke to her gravely. "It's a risky venture, my dear, and if I don't come back, my responsibilities will fall on your shoulders. God bless you, my dear, and you too, Clara! We are in your debt!"

Rothlan was strangely formal as he apologized to Lady Ellan for his treatment of her. He ended, however, by grasping her hands and saying tightly, "If by any chance, I don't return ... I ... I would like you to think well of me ... and Amgarad."

Her eyes glazed with tears as she looked at the unhappy bird perched on his shoulder and she nodded wordlessly. He then bowed low to both her and Clara and waded into the water after the MacArthur. Amgarad, now finally forced to leave his master's shoulder, squawked dolefully as he soared into the air and flew over the loch, shrieking his misery, leaving Ellan and Clara facing the empty stretch of water.

"I think we should put some boats out and have the eagles patrol the loch. What if someone has to demerge and swim for it?"

"That's a good idea," approved Clara. "It will give us something to do instead of waiting and worrying."

"I'll call Amgarad!" nodded Ellan. "And we can take one of the boats out ourselves. I'd rather be close by if there is going to be any trouble under the water."

Ellan rowed out into the middle of the loch and for a while, they were content to drift. Clara peered over the side from time to time but the water was still murky from the storm and she couldn't see anything much.

"I've always wondered what it must be like, being a fish," Clara murmured.

Sir James could have told her. Strange but not unpleasant, would probably have been his verdict. At that moment, he was slipping through the water after the others, concentrating hard on not letting his attention stray as it had when he'd lost Jaikie and Hamish over Arthur's Seat! The water was murky and they had to swim close together to keep one another in sight. Sir James knew that they were heading for a specific place, as that afternoon, while the fish were being netted, Rothlan had brought out old maps of the loch and they had pored long over them.

"There's a current that flows round here," Hector had pointed to the eastern end of the loch, "and I'm tempted to think that anything dropped from this end would be pushed against this headland here."

"And if it misses it?" queried Rothlan.

"Aye, there now," muttered Hector. "There's a queer thing. Anything that missed the headland would end up around here," he circled an area at the far end of the loch with his finger.

"What's so strange about that?" Sir James had asked, looking over his shoulder.

Hector had looked at them frowningly. "It's just that it's no' a part of the loch that folk visit ower often. The shore is desolate and overgrown and the pools are poor fishing ..."

"If you ask me," Dougal had murmured, "I'd say that that would be a good place to look."

There was silence as the others had eyed one another speculatively. Rothlan nodded his head slowly. "I agree with Mr MacLeod," he'd said. "It's deep and it's secret. We'll try there first."

Arthur, however, who hadn't had the benefit of studying Lord Rothlan's charts before he set off, had spent many fruitless hours swimming slowly round the brown silt-filled waters, looking for water goblins. Their smell had been unmistakeable and had filled the boathouse. He was sure they were around somewhere.

He swam close to the bottom of the loch as that was where he guessed he would find them. Delving in the silt in Loch Ness had been their favourite occupation and, knowing their narrow, finicky ways, he reckoned that not a lot would have changed. In the event, he smelled them before he saw them and creeping slowly and stealthily along the loch's muddy bottom, managed to remain unobserved. Sidling behind a growth of slimy weed, he peered through its fronds and choked back a gasp of astonishment. Never, not even in Loch Ness, had he seen so many hundreds of water goblins.

In front of him, the bottom of the loch sheered steeply downwards to form a long, deep trench. Water goblins were everywhere, removing bucketful upon bucketful of silt. The water was thick with it. Arthur wished that he could move nearer but, as that was impossible, he wriggled himself gently into the mud so that at least he could find out what was going on.

It was then that he saw the serpent. Its body was as thick as a tree trunk and seemed miles long. He watched awestruck as it moved lazily through the water on the other side of the trench, its great gaping jaws revealing rows of sharp, curved teeth.

I wonder if Rothlan knows that he has one of those in his loch, was his immediate thought as he waited for the water goblins to notice the creature and swim for their lives. This, as it happened, proved a non-event as the only notice they took of the monstrous creature was to redouble their already frantic efforts to shift the silt from the bottom of the trench. It was then that he realized that the serpent was their master.

Arthur moved his head a fraction to avoid a rock that was digging into his chin and watched as a shoal of fish swam overhead. Now Arthur did not know a lot about trout but he knew that they didn't swim in shoals. Neither, as far as he was aware, did they wear gold nose-rings.

The fish, as well they might, scattered at the sight of the serpent and the water goblins. It was Sir James

who, with a racing heart, dived hastily for the cover
of the nearest patch of greenery, unaware that he was
quivering with fear in a clump of weeds just beside
Arthur's left eye. His fear was excusable as he was, at
that moment, feeling more than slightly vulnerable.
As far as he was concerned, the sight of the teeth on
the serpent totally overshadowed the discovery of the
water goblins!

Arthur, however, afraid that the fish might draw
attention to his hiding place, opened his eye wide and
glowered at it furiously in an attempt to scare it. In
this he succeeded beyond his wildest dreams. Indeed,
he almost gave Sir James a heart attack. Sir James,
however, once recovered from the shock, breathed a
sigh of relief, for he had not forgotten his first sight of
Arthur's wonderful eyes. Help, it would seem, was at
hand! Fired with new hope, he promptly did a nifty bit
of back-paddling.

"Arthur!" he hissed in the dragon's ear.

Arthur froze! He couldn't believe it. Unable to move
his chin for the piece of rock, he opened his eyes and
looked at the fish again.

"I'm Sir James," hissed the fish. "We're here with
the MacArthur. We're looking for Prince Kalman and a
crown. A Turkish crown."

Arthur waited until the serpent had swum past
before he hissed back. "Is it stuck about with rubies?"

"How the ... how should I know?" hissed back Sir
James.

Arthur looked down his long nose. "Because I've just
noticed that my chin is stuck between something that's
absolutely plastered with rubies!"

Sir James swam carefully forward among the weeds
and, sure enough, jutting up from among their roots
were the prongs of a crown. It was black with age but

Arthur had been right about one thing; it was studded all over with rubies and his scaly chin seemed to be stuck firmly between two of its prongs.

Never in his life had Sir James felt so helpless. He longed to have the use of his arms so that he could prise the crown free of the mud; for it wouldn't, he felt, take much of an effort to jerk it loose. He glanced round but as the rest of the trout had wisely disappeared at the sight of the massive serpent, he realized that he and Arthur were on their own.

"Arthur, listen carefully. I can't do a thing! As you see, I've no hands at the moment! It's all up to you now! Try lifting your head slowly so that you can free the crown from the weeds. Then we'll see if we can get away!"

They waited until the serpent had swum past them to the other end of the trench before Arthur started to pull his head back. The crown moved and lifted free but it took some of the weeds with it.

"Stop there, Arthur," Sir James hissed. "I'll try and get rid of the weeds!"

Nudging them with his nose, however, did not the slightest bit of good and once more they rested as the serpent glided slowly past.

It was at this moment that Sir James made a serious error of judgment. The size and weight of the serpent and its lazy movements in the water had unconsciously fostered the idea that it was a relatively slow-moving creature.

"The crown is stuck to your chin, Arthur. Why don't you just take off for the surface of the loch and fly into the air!"

Now, although Arthur had a much better understanding of the serpent's abilities than Sir James did, he could think of no alternative. In the past he had heard vague stories of the Sultan of Turkey's crown and knew only too well the importance of keeping it out of Kalman's hands. Indeed, he had a shrewd suspicion that Kalman *was* the monstrous serpent that so assiduously patrolled the trench.

They waited until the serpent had reached the furthest end of its beat before Arthur rocketed upwards.

He almost made it to the surface, but not quite.

The serpent swung round in a tight turn that would have put an Edinburgh taxi driver to shame and moved like lightning. Indeed, Sir James had never seen anything move with such speed in his life. The muscles of the great creature powered it through the loch. It streaked upwards after the dragon in a swirl of water that knocked Sir James sideways and its great jaws clamped on one of Arthur's legs as he broke the surface, wings flapping wildly.

32. Healing Hexes

From their rowing boat, Lady Ellan and Clara turned as they heard the sudden splash as Arthur reared out of the waters of the loch. He was roaring with fury and pain as he tried frantically to rise into the air. His wings flapped, but to no avail, and it was then that they saw the massive head of the serpent, clamped to one of his legs. Still Arthur struggled to rise but the weight of the serpent was dragging him inexorably down into the water.

It was then that Amgarad and his eagles decided to take a hand in the matter. Arthur saw them coming and, thinking them his enemies, knew that he was lost. He redoubled his efforts to get clear of the water but the serpent held on grimly. The eagles continued their swoop towards the water and much to Arthur's surprise dug their claws not into him, but into the serpent. Flapping their great wings and pecking holes in the beast with their sharp beaks, they added their efforts to his and, gripping the slimy creature as best they could, desperately started to drag the serpent out of the loch.

Clara and Ellan grasped one another's hands as, slowly but surely, the serpent was lifted, still struggling furiously, from the water. The end, however, came suddenly as, realizing that it was doomed, the serpent released Arthur's leg from its vice-like grip and arching in agony gave a spasmodic jerk that threw off the eagles. Its lashing tail, however, struck Arthur's head, loosening the crown from his jaw and Clara and Ellan could only watch in horror as, with a tremendous splash, both the serpent and the crown fell back into the waters of the loch.

Knocked almost unconscious by the vicious blow from the serpent's tail, Arthur, too, tumbled from the sky and, as the eagles swooped and dived helplessly overhead, crashed, with a terrific splash, back into the loch. Ellan rowed swiftly towards him as he surfaced and lay, flapping feebly in the water, blood pouring from the terrible gash on his head and from his injured leg.

As she leant over the side of the boat to reach the injured dragon, Amgarad swept across the water to land on Clara's shoulder. She grimaced as she felt his claws penetrate her jacket but Amgarad was careful not to scratch her and anyway, she reflected, her jacket was so filthy that a few extra tears and scratches were not going to matter. Secretly, too, she was proud that he had come to her at all, as he was Lord Rothlan's bird.

A shout from the shore made them turn their heads. Clara saw her father waving and the others clambering out of the shallow waters onto the shores of the loch.

"Tell them that Arthur is injured and needs help, Amgarad," Ellan gasped as she desperately tried to hold the dragon's head above the water. "I can't hold him for much longer."

Rothlan's men on the shore, however, had witnessed the struggle of the giant creatures and knowing that their help would be needed, had launched their boats and were already half-way between them and the shore. As Amgarad flew off, Clara reached over the side of the boat to help Ellan. Blood was everywhere and Arthur seemed to be slipping in and out of consciousness as his immense weight threatened to drag both them and their boat into the depths of the loch. Clara hung on desperately, blessing the power of her firestone that seemed to be giving her superhuman strength.

The boats, actually, arrived just in time. The men in them were quick to assess the situation and dived into the water clutching the ends of fishing nets that unrolled behind them as they dived underneath the dragon. They looped the nets under Arthur and fastened them to the boats on either side so that they could be drawn taut, thus lifting his body to the surface of the water. Clara and Ellan watched as they made the nets fast and only then rowed to the shore where Rothlan and the MacArthur waited anxiously. Once Arthur's weight was spread across the net, it was possible to row him to the shallow, sandy shore of the loch but it was an operation that took time and had to match the pace of the swimmers who swam alongside him, keeping his head above the surface.

Clara stood clutching her father's hand as she watched the men manoeuver their boats so that the net deposited Arthur at the water's edge. Tears welled in her eyes and spilled down her cheeks as she glanced at Ellan who stood as white as a sheet beside Arthur. Both had had a close-up view of his dreadful injuries and Clara knew instinctively that he had been badly hurt. She had grown very fond of him and the knowledge that he might well die from the terrible wound was almost too much to bear. Indeed, the great dragon looked dead already, lying as he did, still and unmoving, half in and half out of the water. She watched dully as Lord Rothlan, kneeling by his head, placed his hands on the horrendous gash that gouged his forehead and murmured the words of a spell.

The result was nothing short of fantastic. Even as Rothlan straightened and turned to Lady Ellan, Arthur showed signs of life. His body stirred slightly and his claws dug into the sandy foreshore. And as Ellan ran forward, he opened his eyes and struggled feebly.

"Stay still, Arthur," Lord Rothlan warned. "Let me attend to your leg before you do anything else." Again Rothlan murmured the words of a spell and the ragged gashes of the serpent's teeth magically disappeared.

Ellan couldn't hide her delight and gratitude. "Lord Rothlan!" she cried, holding her hands out to him. "How can I thank you? You have given us back our most precious possession! Arthur is dear to us all!"

"Aye," the MacArthur added, "the hill wouldn't be the same without Arthur. We just can't thank you enough!"

Everyone crowded round to look at Arthur and, as he got unsteadily to his feet, a burst of clapping and cheering rang out. Clara couldn't believe her eyes. Arthur's head now showed no sign of his dreadful injuries and already he was regaining his strength. She clapped delightedly as he managed to heave himself out of the water and gamely struggled up the grassy bank with Lord Rothlan and Lady Ellan hovering protectively on either side of him.

"Sir James!" Arthur said, stopping suddenly and looking around. "Where is he?"

It was only then that everyone realized that in the excitement of Arthur's fight with the serpent, no one had noticed that Sir James had not returned.

"He hasn't come back yet. Why?" asked Rothlan sharply.

"The trench ... it was full of water goblins. They ... they must have seen him when I headed for the surface!"

There was a sudden silence as everyone turned to look anxiously over the empty loch.

"He'll be all right. Don't worry," Rothlan said. "I took the precaution of putting a spell on our trout before we left. The water goblins would not be able to hurt him. And," he said, suddenly stern, "while I remember, I might just as well hex that nasty little lot out of Jarishan for ever!"

He straightened his arm and called some strange-sounding words across the loch. Nothing seemed to happen and, seeing Clara's doubtful look, he raised his eyebrows in amusement. "I am, actually, a very good magician," he assured her, and laughed as she blushed in confusion.

"I didn't mean to be rude," she stammered.

She was saved from further embarrassment by the sound of running feet as Neil and Archie came running down to the shore. They stopped dead as they saw Lord Rothlan in the group around Arthur.

"Neil!" Clara cried in relief, running to hug him, "Neil, it's all right. We're all friends now! Oh, I'm so glad that you've woken up at last."

Full of concern, Archie ran straight to Arthur. "Arthur! Are you all right? What's been happening?"

The MacArthur stepped forward and laid a hand on his shoulder. "A lot happened when you were asleep, lad. Lord Rothlan is our enemy no longer and indeed, has just saved Arthur's life. I'll leave Arthur to tell you of his amazing adventure but Rothlan says he needs to rest now. Actually he's just told me that his stables will house Arthur quite comfortably so you can help Hector get him up to the castle."

It was then that Sir James emerged from the shallow water and waded onto the shingle, dripping wet and totally weary.

"Are you all right, James?" MacLeod ran towards him and grasped him by the arm. "We were worried about you!"

"At one stage I was worried about myself," Sir James admitted. "After Arthur took off, I rather lost my bearings. Since then, I think I must have been swimming round in circles! I'm totally exhausted!" He gave a heartfelt sigh of relief as he walked up to the dragon.

"Thank goodness you're okay, Arthur. I heard the tremendous commotion that was going on at the top of the water but, quite frankly, there wasn't a lot I could do to help. I can't tell you how relieved I was when the serpent fell back into the water! Did you get away with the crown?"

There was a dreadful silence at his words as, apart from Clara and Ellan, no one else knew that the crown had been found.

Arthur shook his head sadly. "In the struggle, the serpent's tail hit me in the face," he explained, "and knocked the crown off my chin. It ... it fell back into the loch."

Everyone turned and looked searchingly over the loch. Its bland surface, now placid and unruffled, told them nothing, and Arthur's voice when he spoke was barely more than a whisper. "I think ... I'm afraid Prince Kalman might have it!"

33. Prince Kalman

Prince Kalman did, indeed, have the crown.

As the serpent crashed back into the loch, the prince left its writhing body and hurriedly merged into the first water goblin he came across. Leaving the hapless monster thrashing in its death agonies, Prince Kalman swam swiftly away, his mind on the crown; for he had glimpsed it falling through the air and knew it must be nearby.

Frantically, he swam backwards and forwards through the murky water until he saw it, resting in all its glory on the sandy floor of the loch. Triumph surged through him as he swam up to it and grasped it firmly in his webbed hands. It was his! The crown was his at last!

Water goblins, however, are not large creatures and although they can swim like fish, are not physically strong. To his total frustration, the prince found that he could barely move the crown off the bed of the loch, far less carry it to the surface. Grimly he pulled, tugged and heaved but the best he could do was lift it a few feet before it fell back to the ground. Indeed, he was on the point of total exhaustion when he suddenly found himself drawn inexorably upwards in a swirling eddy of water that shot him unceremoniously onto the hillside at the side of the loch. Choking and spluttering, he demerged from a very surprised water goblin and saw, to his relief, that his hands still gripped the crown.

It took him a few seconds to work out what must have happened and an evil grin spread over his face as he realized that he probably had Lord Rothlan to thank for such an amazing turn of fortune. Who else, after all, would want to hex the water goblins out of the loch?

He threw a mocking salute in the direction of the castle as he rose to his feet. He knew, however, that he was not yet out of danger and, hurriedly scanning the sky for eagles, moved into the shelter of some trees. Seconds later, Kitor swooped down to land on his shoulder.

"You found it, Master!" the crow gasped, his eyes popping out of his head at the sight of the jewelled crown that Kalman held so firmly.

The prince stood straight, tall and triumphant. "It is mine at last!" he said, holding it up in front of him. "Look on it well, Kitor! My father's gift to the Meridens! The world will know our name! With the power of this crown I can rule Scotland!" He laughed excitedly. "But what am I saying?" he smiled. "With the power of this crown, I will rule the world!"

"Not if Rothlan's eagles catch you," snapped Kitor in sudden alarm. "Look at them rising from the walls of the castle! They are going hunting, Master, and they are hunting us!"

As the screams of the eagles echoed across the loch, the prince thrust the crown inside the folds of his black coat and edged deeper into the trees. "I must merge with something, Kitor. Quickly! I can't be caught now!"

"There are red deer in one of the hollows further up the hill, Master," Kitor said. "Keep to the trees and we will come close to them."

Kalman moved swiftly towards the shallow hollow that held the grazing deer. Gently, he eased himself close to an ancient hind that stood apart from the rest of the herd, her ears flickering suspiciously at every movement of the heather. Softly he breathed the words of a spell and even as she turned her head in alarm, he held her in thrall and, step by step, drew her towards him until he could merge with her safely.

"Good luck with the eagles, Kitor," were his master's last, mocking words as the hind ambled off slowly to rejoin the herd.

Although Kitor's eyes narrowed at the callous remark, he was wise enough not to comment. He heaved a sigh as he slid into the shelter of a cleft branch and huddled out of sight; for the eagles, he knew, would not penetrate the forest. It would only be when darkness fell that he would venture forth, but not before!

Night was falling as the MacArthur, Rothlan, Sir James and the children made their way back to the castle in straggling groups with Arthur at their head. When they reached its walls, they found everyone gathered outside to welcome them and a great cheer arose from both the MacArthurs and Rothlan's men.

Inside the castle, the delicious smell of food that rose from the kitchens made everyone appreciate how ravenously hungry they were.

Clara was shown to one of the bedrooms where a servant brought her a bowl of hot water, soap and a towel and took away her clothes. Laid on the bed was a long dress of fine wool with a matching wrap of the same material.

"I hope it fits you, miss," said Hector's wife entering the room. "It belongs to my niece."

"I'm sure it will," said Clara, holding it up. "It's a beautiful dress. I've never had anything as nice to wear in my whole life!"

"Let's see it on then," smiled Ellan as she peeped round the door. She entered the room wearing an elegant high-waisted blue dress and gracefully, turned this way and that to show it off.

Mrs Mackenzie eyed her approvingly as she buttoned Clara into her frock. "It brings out the colour of your eyes, milady!" Then she stood back to admire Clara, as she paraded in front of a mirror. "Ocht! You look lovely, the pair of you," she nodded. "Now, I must go and help attend to the supper. When you're ready just go downstairs, for the master will be waiting."

"It's funny being friends with Lord Rothlan now," mused Clara, sitting at the side of her bed. "I'm not a bit scared of him any more and the way he cured Arthur was wonderful!"

Ellan nodded. "He is our ally now, Clara, against Prince Kalman. For Kalman, you know has the same evil disposition as his father and he will never give up." She strode worriedly around the room. "I do wish I knew what had happened to the crown. If only Kalman doesn't know that it fell back into the loch!"

The sound of voices at the door made them turn. "That sounds like Neil," Clara said, jumping up hurriedly. "I wonder what they've given *him* to wear!"

Neil and Jaikie stood rather awkwardly outside. Both were dressed alike in kilts of Jarishan tartan, ruffled shirts and the green woollen jackets that Rothlan and his men customarily wore. They eyed her rather self-consciously, as did her father, Sir James and Dougal MacLeod when they all met on the stairs but, as their clothes suited their surroundings, she soon became accustomed to them and whispered to Neil that she thought the kilt a big improvement on jeans.

A huge fire blazed in the great hall and after a banquet in which roast pig vied with beef, lamb, haunches of venison and raised pies, they retired once more to the comfort of its armchairs.

It was Lord Rothlan who broke the silence. "Before we discuss the loss of the crown, perhaps we could be told how it was found?"

Sir James answered. "Actually, it was Arthur who found the crown. Purely by accident, as it happened."

The MacArthur snorted. "Very little happens to that crown by accident, Sir James! But go on nevertheless."

"You see, Arthur and I chose the same spot to hide in. He'd spent a lot of time searching the loch before he found the water goblins and it so happened that the crown was among the weeds that fringed their trench. In fact, he managed to get his chin stuck between two of its prongs. That's when I swam into the picture, so to speak."

"What did you do?" asked Rothlan with interest.

"Quite frankly, there isn't a lot you can do when you're a fish," admitted Sir James with a rueful smile. "Really, the only option open to us was to try to get the crown to the surface before the serpent noticed. Arthur almost made it, you know, but never in my life have I seen anything move as fast as that serpent! Anyhow, it has met its end now!"

"It was alive when it fell into the water!" Clara shivered at the memory of its shriek of agony as it fell crashing back into the loch.

Sir James looked at her and his voice was gentle. "It actually fell back into the water in the nick of time, Clara, for by then the water goblins had spotted me. The serpent's return threw them into a panic but the moment they saw that it was injured they set on it!" And although his tone was casual, Sir James knew that he would never forget the thrashing, agonizing end of the serpent.

"Does that mean that Prince Kalman is dead?" asked Neil doubtfully.

Rothlan gave a harsh laugh. "If only it did! Knowing Kalman, I wouldn't bank on it." He rose to his feet and strolled to look out of the windows. "Even now, Amgarad and the eagles are busy patrolling the borders, although I doubt if they will see him, far less catch him. He could merge with anything, bird or beast, and make his escape across the mountains."

"Aye! He's a slippery character that one!" muttered the MacArthur. "But tell me, Sir James, what do you think? Does Kalman have the crown?"

"I honestly don't know," answered Sir James slowly. "I'm tempted to think that he doesn't, but I might well be mistaken."

"We know where it fell," Lady Ellan interrupted. "Surely we could send search parties to see if it's there. Personally though, I'm tempted to leave it where it is."

"You're wrong, Ellan," said the MacArthur, shaking his head. "For good or ill, the crown has to be found. Alasdair will agree with me, I'm sure. It's not the sort of thing one leaves lying around, m'dear."

"You're right, MacArthur," nodded Rothlan. "If it is in the loch, it must be found. If it isn't, then we must inform the Lords of the North."

The MacArthur smiled sourly. "If that doesn't stir them, nothing will! The thought of Kalman in possession of the crown is enough to give them more than a few sleepless nights! He's been trying to become Master of the Council for years!"

"With your permission, MacArthur, perhaps Arthur could stay here for a while and help with the search?" suggested Rothlan. "Archie, too, of course."

"A good idea," approved the MacArthur. "I'm sure they'd be willing to help you in any way they can."

At that moment, Amgarad flew in through the open window and perched on the arm of his master's chair.

Rothlan's face was transformed as he looked at his now majestic eagle. "Well, Amgarad?" he smiled, "what have you to report?"

"The water goblins have left Jarishan, Master. Their fear is terrible and they are following the sheep tracks to the north. But of Prince Kalman there is no sign at all."

Rothlan nodded his head. "It is as I expected. You have done well, Amgarad. Now that darkness has fallen I will put the magic shield around us again. Tonight we can all sleep in safety."

34. A Matter of Time

The next morning saw the MacArthur and his men preparing to make the journey back to Edinburgh. Although there was much hustle and bustle outside the walls of the castle, breakfast in the great dining room was a quiet meal with everyone busy with their own thoughts. Sir James and Dougal MacLeod would have liked to stay longer but thoughts of the Tattoo were pressing. Neil and Clara, however, were of one mind; they wanted to stay in Jarishan forever. Neil longed to explore the stretches of woodland that lay on the far shores of the loch and Clara wanted to see the red deer on the mountains. Lady Ellan, too, would have liked to spend a few more days in the country as her mother's family was Highland and she was more at home above the ground than in the dark caverns that lay under Arthur's Seat. She did not voice her thoughts, however, as she knew how much her father relied on her.

"You are all very quiet this morning," Rothlan observed as a servant removed his empty plate and poured him a cup of coffee. "Are you not looking forward to returning to Edinburgh?"

"No," said Clara truthfully, "we like it here."

Rothlan glanced around the table. "And I," he laughed, "am in love with the hustle and bustle of the city. Edinburgh caught my heart but when you leave I know that much of my time will have to be spent repairing the castle. I'm hoping though that if everything is finished by the spring, you could all come up and spend a few weeks here at Jarishan."

There was a delighted murmur of thanks from everyone around the table. Neil and Clara were ecstatic. "That'd be great! Thank you, Lord Rothlan!" Neil's eyes were shining. "Do you think Hector would take us into the mountains to see the deer?"

"I'm sure he would!" Rothlan smiled.

"And I'll see Amgarad again," smiled Clara happily.

"We will come with pleasure," said the MacArthur, "and you know that you are always welcome to stay with us in Edinburgh. If Kalman causes trouble then we may have to meet up at some point. Anyway, there are always the crystals."

The knowledge that they would return to Jarishan made their parting less difficult. Final goodbyes were said as the magic carpets were summoned. Arthur and Archie, who had been quite willing to stay and help Rothlan search the loch, wished everyone a safe journey and all too soon, it seemed, they were in the air again, flying back to Edinburgh.

Jarishan seemed empty after the MacArthurs had left but, as he had said, Lord Rothlan had many things to attend to. His plans for the castle, however, had to be put on hold when the Lords of the North, anxious to hear what Prince Kalman had been up to, summoned him to appear before their Council.

Amgarad, too, had plans. With Archie's help, the remains of his burnt-out nest were swept away and he built himself a new one in the topmost tower of the castle. The thorny scrub of the winter years had disappeared from the hillside and for his new nest he used heather and soft bracken. When it was built, he lined it with the fur that Clara had given him. It was the one she had wrapped him in when he had lost his feathers and, during the cold winter months when the wind howled and blizzards blew over Jarishan, he snuggled, grateful and contented, in its warm, comfortable depths.

Arthur and Archie stayed on at Jarishan until it became obvious that they were not going to find the Sultan's Crown. Archie had helped Arthur in his search but, as day after day passed and they returned empty-handed to the castle, Lord Rothlan finally called a halt for, as he said, had the crown lain where it had fallen, it would surely have been found within the first few days of their search. Either Prince Kalman had it, they decided, or the crown itself did not want to be found. Rothlan bade them farewell with a shade of worry clouding his eyes. Could Kalman have taken the crown after all?

Although they were sad to leave Lord Rothlan and Amgarad, it was also true that both Arthur and Archie missed the company of the MacArthurs and were anxious to hear what was going on in Edinburgh.

Many weeks had passed since the others had left on their carpets and, indeed, for Sir James, MacLeod, the Ranger and his children, it had been a strange return to Edinburgh. So accustomed had they become to magic carpets and dragons that the ordinariness of everyday life seemed dull in the extreme. The weather didn't help either as Edinburgh was blanketed in a morning mist so thick that, had the carpets not known their way, they could have missed the hill entirely.

"Wow!" said Neil when he finally scrambled off his carpet inside the hill, "did you see the mist? It's almost as thick as the one that was on the hill the first time we met Amgarad. Doesn't that seem ages ago?"

Clara, who had cried and hugged Amgarad before she left, shook her head in disbelief. "I can't believe they were ... are ... the same bird. I adore Amgarad now."

"He adores you too, next after Lord Rothlan that is!"

"Well, you two," said Sir James, walking up to them. "It's strange being back inside the hill again, isn't it?"

Clara looked round doubtfully. "It's not the same as before, though. Then we were starting out on an adventure and now nothing exciting will ever happen again."

"Well I don't know about that! I still have the Tattoo to contend with this evening," said Sir James with a smile. "At least," he said slyly, "there won't be any pigeons around to spook the walkways, which is a relief!" They were still laughing when they saw Dougal MacLeod and the Ranger making their way towards them through the melee of carpets that were arriving all the time.

"I've just been wondering about the Tattoo tonight, James." MacLeod said worriedly.

The MacArthur heard him as he came striding over, still heady with relief at the way things had gone at Jarishan.

"Don't worry about the Tattoo at all, either of you! I have everything in hand. Believe me it will go brilliantly."

"The statues in George Street," said MacLeod suddenly. "People will be wondering ..."

"I assure you, Dougal," said the MacArthur, "that when you next walk down George Street, you will find that the statues are there. As far as the people of Edinburgh are concerned, they will never have disappeared!"

"But they did," said a frowning Dougal. "I hexed them!"

"And I will hex them back again. Don't worry," he smiled. "It'll all work out in the end. See now, what I've done is this," said the MacArthur, drawing them round. "During the journey back I gave the matter some thought and I decided that the best thing to do would be to cast a memory spell so that the days of the past will only be real for us, and no one else."

"You can do that?" Sir James looked at him sharply.

"Aye! The firestones, Sir James, have given us tremendous power for good. Nobody will know the difference, I assure you."

"What a relief that is!" sighed Dougal. He glanced around at them all. "MacArthur," he said, shaking him by the hand, "you're a magician and a half! A magician and a half!"

The MacArthur proved true to his word. The first thing Dougal MacLeod did was to drive to the middle of town and check up on the statues in George Street. There they stood; solid as rocks! Dougal vowed there and then, never to utter a word against them again.

While memory spells had their advantages, there was, however, more than one downside. Ranger MacLean realized it when he got home and found that his wife had no memory of anything that had happened.

"You must remember Neil coming home that night with his jacket all torn," he said, "and I told you how we met the MacArthurs and were going to Jarishan!"

"No, I don't," she insisted, looking quite upset. "I don't remember anything at all! I think you're having me on!"

"Well," said Neil, meeting his father's glance doubtfully, "at least we know that the MacArthur's spell is working!"

Clara saw tears in her mother's eyes. "Mum," she said, "we wouldn't fool you, you know that!"

"Magic carpets!" Mrs MacLean muttered as she went on laying the table for lunch. "You've been reading too many of these fantasy adventure stories, Clara."

"Hang on," Neil said excitedly, "we can still call our carpets, can't we?"

His father's face cleared and he smiled suddenly. "Brilliant, Neil!" he said, turning to his wife. "Come into the garden, Janet and we'll show you that what we've been saying is the truth!"

Mrs MacLean watched as they clapped their hands and said "carpet" in loud voices. She looked doubtfully around as nothing happened and would have gone back indoors if her husband hadn't gripped her arm.

"Trust me, Janet! They'll be here in a minute!"

Then, as Mrs MacLean looked on in amazement, three carpets sailed smoothly over the garden wall to hover gently in front of them.

Neil clambered onto his carpet and his mother gasped as he disappeared. "You'd better take Mum for a ride on your carpet, Dad," he said, jumping back down onto the path. "She'll never believe in magic otherwise."

"Get on the carpet, Janet," urged the Ranger, helping her onto it and holding her tightly. Neil looked at Clara and grinned as the carpet disappeared and they heard their mother laughing excitedly as it circled the garden.

"Well, Mum," Clara ran to hug her mother as she appeared again, "do you believe us now?"

"I do," she said as they trooped back into the house. "Really, John, this is fantastic!"

It was while they were having lunch round the kitchen table that Clara suddenly had a dreadful thought.

"Dad!" she said, sitting bolt upright in her chair. "Dad! If ... if Mum couldn't remember a thing about what's been going on then it means that poor little Mischief will still be a stray! Mr MacGregor won't remember having taken her in!"

The Ranger looked at his wife, who had just finished hearing all about Archie, Mischief and Mr MacGregor. "Would you mind giving a home to a wee cat?" he asked.

She looked round the table at their anxious faces, still more than a bit baffled at the stories they were telling her. Faeries in Arthur's Seat were one thing but dragons and great eagles were quite another. Thank goodness, she thought, that it was only a cat they wanted to bring into the house.

"Of course, you can bring it here," she said weakly.

The Ranger smiled at Neil and Clara. "Why don't you go up to the school this afternoon then and see if you can find her," he said. "Take a big cardboard box to carry her in."

"Can we really, Dad?" Neil jumped to his feet in excitement. "I'm sure she'd like being with us better than old MacG ... sorry, Mr MacGregor. Not that there's anything wrong with Mr MacGregor but a school's not as comfortable as a home, is it?"

"No, it isn't," smiled his mother, "you go and fetch her!"

After lunch, Neil and Clara hurriedly made their way to school. Mr MacGregor, who was standing in the playground amid a pile of boxes, did not notice them at first as he was busily consulting a clip-board.

"Hello, Mr MacGregor!" Neil greeted him tentatively.

"Hello there, you two! Tired of being on holiday already, are you?"

"Being on holiday's great," Clara assured him, "but we've really come for that little cat. You know, the black and white one!"

"Oh ... it! It's somewhere around, I dare say."

"Dad said we could give it a home," explained Neil. "So we've come to fetch it."

"Aye, well! It'll put on weight if it goes to your house. A grand cook, your mother!"

"We'll just go round the playground to look for her then, if that's all right with you."

"Aye! You do that. And tell your dad that I was asking for him. We'll have to get together soon. I've a big darts match coming up!"

Neil and Clara walked round the playground and, sure enough, there was Mischief perched on the playground wall.

"Mum's going to freak!" Neil said worriedly. "She's expecting a decent-looking animal and Mischief isn't even half-decent. She's scraggy!"

But Mrs Maclean and the little cat got on very well together and it did not take Mischief long to become part of the MacLean family. Everyone spoiled her and as the weeks went by she put on weight and the memory of past hardships faded. This was especially true when the weather became really cold and she stretched blissfully on the rug in front of the living room fire and slept the day away.

35. Here Be Dragons

Clara and Neil visited the hill once or twice after their return but somehow it just wasn't the same without Arthur and Archie. They went back to school at the end of August and were soon laden with homework, book reports and project work. One cold morning, when they were sitting on a low wall in the playground, eating their sandwiches, Neil saw old MacGregor walking towards the gate.

"Congratulations, Mr MacGregor," he called.

The janny smiled and walked over to them. "Aye! Did ye hear about it, then?"

"Dad told us last night," Clara said. "You won the darts final for the East of Scotland!"

"I did that! And now I'm entered for the Scottish Open Championships!" He looked suddenly worried, for he had not yet come to terms with his quite phenomenal rise to fame in the darts' world. "I'll be up against the big boys then! I hope my luck holds out!"

Neil and Clara exchanged a look that spoke volumes. "Mr MacGregor," said Clara solemnly, "from the way my dad said you played last night — cool as a cucumber and totally sure of yourself — well, we think you're destined to go right to the top. Don't you agree, Neil?"

Neil nodded. "I'm absolutely certain, Mr MacGregor. Believe me; you'll have magic in your fingers! There's no doubt about it! You'll win!"

When the janny had left them to attend to some parents by the gate, Neil and Clara looked at one another.

"The MacArthur really has been busy, hasn't he," Neil remarked.

"Definitely!" nodded Clara.

"I think he's thrown some magic my way as well, you know. I really find school work easy this year."

"So do I. But most of all, I've stopped being afraid of the dark. You've no idea what it was like! At night, even though I knew for sure that there was no one else in the house, I used to be scared to go downstairs for a glass of water. Now I can even see in the dark in a funny kind of way. Like the negative of a photograph."

Two pigeons flew down and hopped over to them. Clara and Neil paid them no attention and went on talking.

"Hi!" said one. "I'm Jaikie!"

"I'm Hamish!" said the other.

"Jaikie! Hamish!" said Neil, his eyes darting round the playground to see who was near, "how wonderful to see you again! Has anything happened?"

"Archie and Arthur are coming back from Jarishan tonight and we're having a big party for them. You are all invited and the MacArthur would like you to pass on the invitation to your father, Sir James, Mr MacLeod and Mr Todd at the distillery. Oh, and Lady Ellan sends her regards and says to please bring your mother as well."

"Brilliant!" said Neil, who had not really appreciated how dull life had become without the MacArthurs, "Mum will be delighted!"

It proved a tremendous party. Magic was in the air as they met old friends and talked of their adventures. Arthur and Archie brought news of Jarishan and the best wishes of Lord Rothlan and Amgarad. Lady Ellan hugged Neil and Clara warmly and apologized profusely to Dougal MacLeod for the incident at the Tattoo when he had been so roughly deprived of the firestones.

Everyone made a fuss over Mrs MacLean and although she was a bit apprehensive of Arthur at first, she soon relaxed as she watched her children rush over to the dragon, hug him warmly and pelt him with questions.

The MacArthur beamed happily throughout the evening and, looking round at the assembled gathering, Sir James was very much aware that a little magic had touched all of their lives. The Ranger's work with the police force had earned him well-deserved recognition, Dougal MacLeod had shed his old personality and become something of a wit. Old MacGregor (who had got on very well with the MacArthur during their stay at the school) had become a star in the world of darts, Clara was no longer afraid of the dark, and both she and Neil were making excellent progress at school. As for himself, Sir James smiled as he nursed a wonderful feeling of deep content. Never, in all his days, had he tasted a whisky to equal it. Smooth, rich and utterly glorious, the whisky that he had retrieved from Arthur's lake inside the hill had proved a veritable connoisseur's dream — all twenty thousand gallons of it!

Although he tut-tutted at Sir James's assertion that they all had good cause to be grateful to him the MacArthur was nevertheless pleased that they appreciated his efforts on their behalf. "Ocht, I didn't really do much," he murmured defensively. "Sharpened Neil and Clara's memory a wee bit, and MacGregor's eyesight!"

Dinner was a feast of mammoth proportions and it was only when they could eat no more and reached gratefully for their coffee that the MacArthur told them what had happened after they had left Jarishan.

"You'll be pleased to hear," he said, sitting back in his chair and looking round at them all, "that Lord Rothlan has been accepted back into the world of magic and is again one of the Lords of the North."

An excited murmur of pleasure rippled round the table and Clara clapped her hands. "Fantastic," Sir James smiled. "I'm sure we wish him every success!"

"He is still worried about the crown, of course, and one of the first things he did, was to trace Agnes, the carpet-mender. He found her near Lochinver and brought her back to Jarishan with him. Although she is still afraid of Kalman, he eventually managed to wheedle the whole story out of her. Ellan, as it turned out, was right all along. Kalman had more or less kept Agnes prisoner until she had finished piecing together the shreds of his father's carpet."

"It must have been an enormous job," said Lady Ellan. "It was in tatters! I don't know how she did it!"

Her father nodded. "Joining threads in some places, I should imagine. But when she finally finished stitching it together and the carpet was whole again, it was able to talk. Kalman, Agnes said, was ruthless. He said he's burn it if it didn't tell him what had happened to his father on the night of the storm. At that threat, the carpet, needless to say broke down and told him everything he wanted to know. Prince Casimir, it said, had been terrified, but refused to give the crown up. As the storm carriers homed in on him he used the crown's own magic to tie it to the Meriden family for ever. The carpet didn't know whether or not the spell actually 'took' for Casimir's magic was flawed as he'd cheated to get the crown. Magic can be a funny thing, sometimes."

"I think the carpet was right," Ellan said. "The crown must have had remnants of its own magic left for it didn't fall into Meriden territory, did it? It fell instead into Jarishan."

"So that's how Kalman knew the crown was there," said Neil breathlessly. "And he had to break the shield to get in to find it!"

The MacArthur nodded. "I think it is more than likely that Kalman has the crown although there are no signs yet that he is using it."

"If what Alasdair told us this morning is true, then he might well have started," objected Lady Ellan. "Lord Rothlan told us this morning that Kalman seems to have disappeared. None of the crystals can pick him up and no one seems to know where he is."

"Or what he's up to!" added the MacArthur.

The knowledge that Kalman had the crown threw something of a cloud over the festivities and as they climbed onto their carpets at the end of the evening, their goodbyes were quiet and subdued.

"We'll keep in touch," the MacArthur promised, shaking hands with them all. "Rothlan plans to visit us in the near future and I'm sure he'll want to see you all again. Your carpets will always be ready for you, you know that, don't you?"

As they all got ready for bed, Neil went into the garden to call Mischief in for the night and looked up as he heard the distant sound of an aeroplane as it started to lose height over the city. Watching its lights, he smiled to himself as he remembered Arthur's adventure and wondered what the pilots' reactions had been when they had seen a dragon flying towards them.

Had Neil been in the cockpit of the aircraft, however, he would have been even more amused for, by sheer coincidence, the same two pilots sat at the controls. Neither of them, as it happened, had been in Edinburgh when the MacArthur had used his memory spell and, as a result, it hadn't quite worked as it should have done. They still, therefore, had vague memories of Arthur and as they approached the city, both pilots became noticeably restless and edgy. One leant forward and did his best to look unobtrusively out of the cockpit window while the other scanned the night sky.

"Anything the matter, Jim?"

The co-pilot looked rather shamefaced and shook his head. "I don't know what it is but every time we come in to land at Edinburgh, I get the totally stupid notion that there might be ... dragons around," he admitted.

"Dragons!" echoed the pilot, "did you say dragons?" He shook his head in relief. "Then it isn't only me! Thank the Lord! I honestly thought I was going round the bend! Tell me I wasn't imagining it all! There *was* a dragon, wasn't there!"

"Scarlet and gold," confirmed the other.

"That's right! With the most amazing eyes!"

"Down there! Over Arthur's Seat! I reckon that's where he came from!"

"Arthur's Seat?"

"You know! That hill down there. The one that's shaped like ... like a sleeping dragon!"

They looked at one another in wondering disbelief and some apprehension as the black bulk of the hill loomed darkly against the scatter of bright lights that marked the city.

Nothing, however, was to mar their steady descent that evening. Below the wings of their aircraft, the hill that was shaped like a sleeping dragon lay dark and silent. And in its depths, Arthur slept.

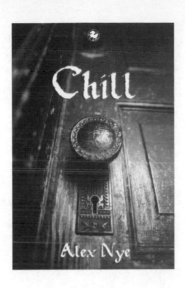

Samuel is trapped by huge snowdrifts in an old,
remote house. And that's not the only thing caus-
ing a cold shiver to creep down his spine. He feels
like the ghostly figure in the locked library has a
message ... but who is it for?

Fiona lives in the big house, but will that help
the two of them to break the curse on her family?
As the ice sets in, they uncover a deadly tale of
betrayal and revenge.

Set on bleak Sheriffmuir near Stirling, this is a
spooky tale of the past coming back to haunt the
present.

Contemporary Kelpies

Fergus can't believe it when his brand-new digital watch starts going backwards. Then he crashes (literally) into gadget-loving Murdo, and a second mystery comes to light — cats are going missing all over the neighbourhood. As the two boys start to investigate, they find help in some unexpected places.

Mike Nicholson won the Kelpies Prize with *Catscape,* his first novel, which is set in his home neighbourhood of Comely Bank, Edinburgh.

Contemporary Kelpies

St Andrews, Fife — not known for its glorious weather, but even so, Josh hadn't expected the sea to start to freeze and ice to creep up the beaches ... His summer holiday isn't looking too promising, especially as his only companions are a strange local girl, Callie, and her enormous dog, Luath.

Then they uncover the journal of an eighteenth-century girl who writes about a Kingdom of Summer, and suddenly find themselves thrown headlong into a storm of witches, ice creatures, magic and the Winter King. A permanent winter threatens unless they can help restore the natural balance of the seasons.

Can they stop the Winterbringers once and for all?

Contemporary Kelpies

Kate and David are eleven-years-old and best of friends, playing football and doing their museum project together. But in Edinburgh, where they live, time is coming unstuck and the past is breaking loose. Old Mr Flowerdew needs their help in the war between the Lords of Chaos and the Guardians of Time, centred around the mysterious Millennium Clock at the Royal Museum.

Can Kate use her grandmother's golden necklace to restrain the power of Chaos, and will David be able to help the Guardians, even if it means losing his mother all over again?

Contemporary Kelpies

It is eighteen months after the events of *The Chaos Clock*, and Kate and David are now at secondary school in Edinburgh. David is struggling to come to terms with his new stepmother, and Kate is being expected to take more responsibility for her younger brother.

But time never stands still for long. They soon become involved in a race to prevent the Lords of Chaos from tricking Erda, the Stardreamer, into losing her power. Even with help from Morgan the Hunter, can they prevent the barriers between times being blown away forever?

Contemporary Kelpies